About the Author

This is Bill's second published story. His first, *Don't Look at Me Like That* (with a foreword by Michael Morpurgo), was a story set at Wick Court Farm (a Farms for City Children farm) in Gloucestershire and raised funds for the charity Farms for City Children.

Bill worked for a long time in primary education in Gloucestershire where he was able to share his love of stories: for him reading the class a book was always a precious time! He also wrote stories for a variety of special school events like productions and assemblies.

He is a Story Teller called 'The Story Traveller' and has performed all over the country telling stories to audiences of all ages. It was following one of his Story Telling visits to a dementia unit that part of this story evolved.

He spends his spare time cycling, bird watching and supporting the mighty Hatters. He volunteers at the wonderful Wick Court Farm taking young people bird watching around the site. He is also Story Teller in Residence at Wick Court sharing stories weekly in the magnificent Round House.

If you want to find out more about The Story Traveller please go to www.thestorytraveller.co.uk

About Jane Fryer

Jane Fryer is a marvellous artist who can turn her pencil and paintbrush to almost anything! She is especially well known throughout the Severn Vale for her individually commissioned paintings celebrating special birthdays and events, etc. As she says: "If you would like me to draw something for you... imagine a list of things all to do with you... all in a painting – wouldn't that be fun?"

This is the second time Jane has collaborated with Bill. She was the illustrator for *Don't Look at Me Like That*.

Jane's number is 01452 741054 or she can be contacted through email janefryer@freeuk.com

PIG
the
Legend

BILL CHURCH
ILLUSTRATIONS BY JANE FRYER

Matador
9 Priory Business Park,
Wistow Road, Kibworth Beauchamp,
Leicestershire. LE8 0RX
Tel: 0116 279 2299
Email: books@troubador.co.uk
Web: www.troubador.co.uk/matador
Twitter: @matadorbooks

ISBN 978 1800463 653

British Library Cataloguing in Publication Data.
A catalogue record for this book is available from the British Library.

Printed and bound by CPI Group (UK) Ltd, Croydon, CR0 4YY
Typeset in 12pt Baskerville by Troubador Publishing Ltd, Leicester, UK

Matador is an imprint of Troubador Publishing Ltd

To carers everywhere.
Thanks!

All proceeds for this book will go to
Alzheimer's Society.

The Alzheimer's Society is the UK's leading
dementia charity. The charity campaigns for
change, funds research to find a cure and supports
people living with dementia today.

In aid of

Contents

Chapter 1

Save Your Bacon!

Abby was looking at different types of leggings on her phone; she was hoping she might persuade her mum to buy her some for the holiday. Her mum had promised her some new stuff. She thought about the colours. *Should I go for pink leggings with mauve stripes down them? Although Bethany will say something like 'pink is so yesterday!' Or should I go for the big yellow spots on black? They make a statement, but yuck – they look awful! It is so hard to decide what I should go for! At least I won't have to wear those stupid school clothes next week.*

She couldn't wait for the holidays to start so she could mess around with her mates.

She now heard the phone ringing and her mother's voice shouting up to her, "Abby, can you answer that, please! I've got my hands all covered in flour!"

She sighed to herself and she walked across the landing from her room to pick up the phone in her mother's room.

"321988, this is Abby speaking…"

A familiar voice with a distinctive burr answered.

"Abby, my dear, it's me, your Granny Sue. I'm sorry, love, but I need to speak to your mum – it is urgent."

"Gran? Are you OK?"

It wasn't like her gran not to chat to her about the world and the universe; she usually could go on and on forever and ever.

"Yes, but it is my George, I must speak to your mum."

Abby felt a sickening jolt in the pit of her stomach. "Grampy? Is he all right?"

"Get your mum, please!"

Abby carried the phone down to her mum in the kitchen. Abby whispered, "Gran, she needs to speak to you urgently. It's Grampy."

Her mum sighed, wiped her hands clumsily on her apron and took the phone. "Hello, Mum, is it Dad again?"

Abby left the kitchen and went into the living room; she flopped down in a chair and started to fiddle with her phone, but she could hear odd snatches of her mum talking to Gran.

"Is he all right now?"

"What did the police say?"

"Oh, Mum, you have managed him on your own for so long and you have been fine, but you do need some help now and you need a rest, otherwise you won't be able to keep going."

"Look, we can be with you at the weekend; Abby will have finished school then so we can help you sort things out."

Abby felt her heart sink; off to Gloucester for a few

days, that certainly wasn't her idea of a holiday. There would be nothing to do there. She would be really bored, and it would mean she wouldn't be able to see her mates. She thought Gloucester was really a bit of a dump.

"Bye now, Mum! You just ring if things get worse."

Her mum now came into the living room and looked forlornly at Abby. "It's your grandad: he went wandering off from the house, dressed only in his pyjamas and his dressing gown. He ended up walking round and round a farm that was a couple of miles from the house. The police found him and took him back home."

Abby looked at her mum; she could see she was close to tears.

Abby now knew she couldn't moan about going to Gloucester, even though she was really disappointed and wouldn't look forward to it. She walked across and threw her arms around her mum. "Don't worry, Mum, what have we got to do to help?"

Her mum sniffed. "I think we might have to look for somewhere for Grampy to go; Gran can't manage him all the time on her own anymore. He needs to be looked after. He is so restless, and he can never settle."

Abby was worried. "Oh, Mum, he can't go somewhere! You know how much he loves his garden and watching the birds on the feeders! He watches them for ages; he has always loved being outside. He will be far worse if he has to leave home."

"I know, I know, but we will need to go and see what can be done. It won't be easy. I'm sorry, love, but we will have to go to Gloucester as soon as the holiday comes. I know there isn't much for you to do there, and you can't go to your dad's because he is away till mid-August. Sorry, but it has to be done!"

Abby sighed. "Whatever… Mum, we must help Gran."

*

A couple of days later Abby was walking round her friend Marie's farm. Abby always enjoyed looking at the animals. Marie had just gone back to the house because she had forgotten her phone.

Abby was feeling really fed up, especially as she had heard a sleepover was being organised on the first weekend of the holiday while she would be in boring old Gloucester! She was moaning to herself out loud, half-talking to the animals. She stopped by the stables and looked at Kenny, a lovely jet-black horse, which was Marie's favourite horse to ride.

"Oh, Kenny, I really don't want to go to Gloucester, but I have to; I wish I could just stay here. I don't know anyone there; it is such a dump and there is nothing to do!"

She heard a strange-sounding high-pitched voice behind her.

"No, you don't want to go! Gloucester is such a dangerous place! It certainly isn't safe!"

She swung round, but was surprised to see no one at all, apart from a large pale-pinkish-coloured pig, with black spots splattered on its body, in the sty opposite.

"Who's there? Hello?"

Her head swivelled rapidly back and forth. There was no sign of anyone; was someone playing a clever trick on her? Who would do that? There was definitely no one there, was there? So, was she imagining it? It was such a strange-sounding voice; it was so high-pitched.

She searched all around the stables and the sty to find whoever it was that was messing about with her. She couldn't find anyone, so she just shrugged her shoulders.

"Must be imagining things! Fancy saying Gloucester is a dangerous place. The only danger I can think of in Gloucester is death by boredom! Watch out because that sneaky boredom creeps up on you and then it takes you over till you can't stop yawning and you are helpless to do anything and so you become bored stiff!"

She had decided to go and look for Marie to see what had happened to her, when the strange voice spoke again.

"Save your bacon! Avoid Gloucester!"

Abby looked all around her but couldn't see anyone apart from Kenny, the horse in the stable, and the pig. The latter seemed to be staring directly at her, although that was difficult as the pig's ears looked like curtains and were halfway across its eyes.

"I could almost think you spoke to me, Mr Pig! Fancy that, pigs talking! I think I must be losing it!"

What happened next astounded Abby. That strange voice really did seem to come from the pig.

"Well, at least I'm not saying we pigs can fly! That would be a really stupid idea. I think I would feel sick if I was up in the air!"

"You, you, you... just spoke to me!"

Abby pinched herself – was she dreaming? She stared hard at the pig. This was suddenly getting a bit

too far-fetched for her. *A talking pig? What is happening to me? Come on, get a grip, Abby!*

Marie's voice now was calling, "Abby, Abby, where are you?"

"I am down by the stable and the sty!"

Abby was relieved to see her friend; she didn't think she would mention that she thought a pig had talked to her. It wasn't the sort of thing you mentioned to people! Imagine that getting round school! Abby was hearing talking pigs! She would never hear the end of it.

The two girls wandered their way to a great oak tree, sat down and watched the swallows swooping and darting low across the field. They munched crisps and chatted. After sitting for a while, Marie said, "Shall we pop back to the house for a drink?"

"OK."

They had just got back to the stable area when Abby realised that she had left her bag dangling from the branch of the oak tree.

"Oh no, I'm an idiot! Marie, I've gone and left my bag on the branch of that tree. I'll just go back and get it and I'll catch you up at the house."

She soon found her bag and started to amble back. Her mind was racing all over the place. She couldn't get rid of the idea that she had thought a pig had spoken to her. *Fancy thinking a pig was talking to me! I think someone was messing around. I bet they are hiding somewhere round here and surely they're laughing at me for falling for it*!

She strolled past the pig, which was lying asleep on its side, its flanks rising and falling as it snored.

She whispered to it, "I really thought you spoke to me earlier. How stupid is that? Me thinking you were a talking pig! It was someone messing around, wasn't it?"

The pig's trotter scratched at the ground and it opened an eye that fixed on her.

Astonishingly it now grunted bad-temperedly some more words at her. "I was merely remarking that Gloucester is a dangerous place. Well at least it is for pigs!"

"You, you, you can really speak. This is amazing! Have you spoken to other people, like Marie? Are you warning me about something?"

The pig's eye was now closed, and its snoring resumed. Abby was unsure what to do; did she really think that the pig had spoken to her? She knew she had a good imagination, she often wrote some inventive stories at school, but this was ridiculous! Thinking she had heard a pig talk to her! So she lingered by the sty, watching the sleeping pig intently. Its flanks were rising and falling with his breathing; was he going to speak again? Now she heard Marie's voice calling from the house, "Abby! Abby, are you coming? Did you find your bag?"

So she turned and made her way back up to the house, feeling confused and worried.

Marie greeted her. "You took your time! Are you OK? You look as white as a sheet!"

Abby lied, "Erm, erm, I just felt a bit dizzy, might be too much sun! Think I'd better go home and lie down for a bit."

She didn't say anything to Marie about what she thought had happened; it wasn't the sort of thing you say to people.

"Oh, by the way your pig was talking to me and it warned me that Gloucester was a dangerous place! Nothing to worry about is it?"

*

Later that night, Abby was lying in her bed thinking about the events of the afternoon. She was trying to be rational, looking for a reason for what had happened.

I suppose I was imagining it all. Maybe because I was worried about Grampy and, of course, I don't want to go to Gloucester, especially for the first weekend of the holiday! They do say your mind can play tricks on you. Yet it did seem so real, it really did seem that it was speaking to me.

At last, she drifted off into an uncomfortable, troubled sleep and she started to dream. Well, it was more like a pig nightmare! She saw pigs of different shapes and sizes everywhere, there were hundreds and hundreds of them, all racing for their lives up Northgate Street in Gloucester. The noise was deafening with the terrible squealing of the pigs. A large man, he was a butcher surely, had a straw boater-type hat perched on his head; he was wearing a blood-stained blue and white striped apron. He was chasing after them waving a great kitchen knife around above his head. He was yelling, "Come on my piggies! I need bacon, I want your bacon! Bacon, bacon, bacon!"

Abby woke up sweating and whimpering with fright. She flicked on her bedside light and looked at her clock; it was 3.15am. She got up and wandered over to the window. She spoke quietly, "Why on earth am I now thinking about pigs all the time? I'm even having nightmares about pigs!"

She half-expected to see pigs flying past her window. After a little while managing not to see any flying pigs she went back to bed. She made up her mind that she would go back to Marie's house, walk through the farm and visit that pig again, just to reassure herself that her imagination was not really running away with her, because pigs can't talk, can they? She soon fell asleep and she couldn't remember any other dreams the next morning; but she did remember that she was going to pop round to Marie after school.

She told Marie that she wanted to take some pictures of the animals because she wanted to make a special card for her grandad; he loved animals, especially pigs.

"Of course, you can, but do you mind if I don't come down with you? Mum needs me to help her get ready for our farm open day, so we are going to design a poster after school."

Abby was actually relieved that Marie wouldn't be with her, as it meant she would be free to try and talk to the pig. As she made her way down to the stables and the sty, she thought to herself, *Talk to a pig? Fancy me going to try and talk to a pig! Not sure what is happening; perhaps it is because I'm so worried about Grampy that my imagination is running away with me. I know he always has liked pigs.*

She spoke gently to the horse. "Hello, Kenny, look what I've brought you, half of a lovely apple to munch. The other half is for you, Mr Pig!"

While the animals munched away, Abby snapped a few photos of the two animals.

"Well, Mr Pig, are you going to speak to me today?"

The pig snorted and continued to gobble up the last traces of the apple.

Nothing happened, not a word from the pig.

Abby hovered around the animals for a while but eventually decided it wasn't going to speak to her, so she turned to make her way back home. She had only taken a few steps when a squeaky voice seemed to drift around her.

"Gloucester is no good for us. Save my bacon, please!"

She wheeled round in a flash and moved back towards the pig. She was also looking around to see if there was anyone playing around with her.

Her face contorted with puzzlement. "Stop messing! Is it really you, Mr Pig? Or am I hearing things?"

The pig had now flopped down and was dozing off.

As Abby just stood and stared at the sleeping pig, she heard Marie call her from further up the path.

"Did you take your pictures, Abby?"

Abby looked towards Marie and nodded.

Marie looked at her friend.

"Are you all right, Abby? It looks like you have seen a ghost. You said you felt unwell yesterday."

Abby smiled weakly. "I'm OK and, yeah, got some photos. I was just leaning over the gate to get shots of the pig, and I was twisting my head!"

"He's a funny old thing, old Herbert. I think he is a real character." She now lowered her voice to a whisper and held a hand to her mouth. "Dad says he will have to go at the end of the month."

Abby now blurted out, "Oh no, he can't, can he?"

"We are a small farm, that is what happens, Abby. It's life! I like Herbert, he is good company, and I don't want to lose him! But that is how it is!"

Abby now was in a blind panic. "Where does he go?"

"Dad might take him to him to market or just sell him to the local abattoir."

Abby looked back at Herbert; she didn't want this to happen, but what could she do? Just at that moment the pig opened his eyes and he appeared to wink at Abby. She was convinced there was something special about this animal and surely, he needed protecting. The story *Charlotte's Web*, that she loved to read when she was younger, now floated into her mind. *Wilbur got saved by a spider, I wonder if I can save old Herbert? Don't think I can spin webs!*

Chapter 2

Lincolnshire
(May 1944)

In a Lincolnshire field there was a flurry of activity as jeeps and trucks raced between the parked squadron of green-and-brown-camouflaged Lancaster bombers. Skylarks trilled their songs from the edge of the field, just faintly heard above the busy bustling noises. Preparations were underway, engineers were checking over the planes while their deadly cargoes were being loaded. The crews were now driven out following their briefing. In the twilight Sergeant Tom Brown fiddled nervously with his flying suit. It was his first operational flight; he hadn't been able to relax at all and he was struggling to urinate on the tail wheel for luck. Everybody else had done their bit! They had laughed nervously at him.

"Come on man, we don't want any bad luck!"

At last the job was done, and he now clambered up into the aircraft, hauling his way to his gun turret. He nervously felt his mask, his other hand unconsciously touching his lucky rabbit's foot. He made a thorough check of his guns and ammunition. He then waited as radio commands were issued, crackling through his flying helmet. Finally, he could see the propellers begin to shake, as the Rolls Royce engines bellowed into action, rocking the whole plane into life. Tom could see

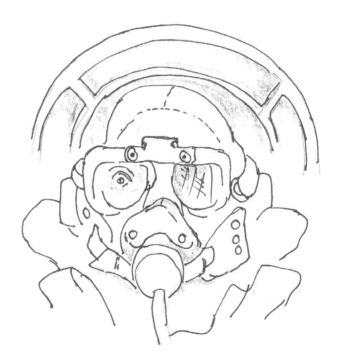

other planes slowly lumbering from their parking slots as they taxied into their take-off positions. His plane, M for Michael, moved laboriously into position. One after the other they accelerated across the field, eating up the grass and gradually lifting slowly up into the darkening skies. Tom's stomach lurched; he gripped the rabbit's foot tightly. He could soon see the reflection of the water in the gloom below as they flew across the sea. He heard the skipper over the intercom.

"Now flying at 10,000 feet and climbing, so you will need your masks on now, gentlemen. Let's hope for all our sakes they work!"

The plane began to climb steadily, and Tom fixed his mask over his face. The temperature soon plummeted, and he was glad of the electric circuit in his suit to give him some warmth. Tom could see many dark shapes in the sky, the mass of the many Lancasters surrounding them as they flew towards the enemy coastline. Once again, the intercom burst into life, and it was a message for him.

"Mid gun, feeling OK? Keep those eyes peeled, please. Watch above us for any bandits. Brace yourselves boys, enemy coastline up ahead. It's going to be hot!"

Tom looked up and saw another Lancaster immediately above them; then, as he looked forward, he could make out the black coastline racing towards them. There were plumes of red and yellow filling the sky ahead.

"Flak up ahead!"

His hands trembled, and it wasn't the cold. Now they were flying over land and flak was all around them, roaring past the aircraft and exploding. The plane was buffeted, and it wobbled erratically.

"Taking evasive action, we are on a zigzag path."

Tom was fascinated by the red and yellow explosions that looked strangely beautiful and bewitching, despite their deadly intent. Mini black clouds appeared everywhere between the planes. Searchlights poured light into the black sky, trying to fix a plane in their trap like an illuminated spider's web. Tom's eyes were blinded by the searing light. The plane up on their starboard side burst into flames and spiralled out of control. On and on they flew, closing in remorselessly on their target. He now heard the navigator's voice.

"Should be over the target in five minutes."

Chapter 3

Boring, Boring Gloucester?

School had finished the next day and Abby and her mum set off to Gloucester. She settled down for the long journey on the motorway and then it was across country. She always liked it when they came over those lovely green rounded Cotswold hills and she could see the snaking silvery great river below. Every time she saw it the colour of the River Severn seemed to be different.

As they neared the city, she saw a field full of pigs and rounded little huts scattered all across it. Everything that had occurred at Marie's farm came flooding back. So why had she thought the pig had warned her about Gloucester? She knew these pigs were Gloucester Old

Spots, just like the one at Marie's. She gulped as they sped past the field of pigs; she realised these poor pigs wouldn't be around much longer. She shivered at the thought of poor old Herbert at Marie's and hoped that he would still be there when she got back from Gloucester. She needed to think of something else.

At last they arrived at her grandparents' house.

They were greeted warmly by Abby's grandmother. "How's Dad, Mum?"

Abby's grandmother shook her head and pointed to the house.

Abby went in, to find Grampy looking out of the window; he held a small plastic pig toy in one hand. Abby rushed to him and threw her arms around him and pressed her face into his chest. She then took a step back and looked at her grandfather. "Hello, Grampy, how are you?"

Her grandfather looked at her and smiled. "Hello!"

"It's me! Abby!"

"Hello!"

"What are you doing with that pig, Grampy?"

"Mustn't hurt the piggies! Mustn't hurt the piggies!"

Abby's mum came into the room, gave her dad a cuddle and then helped him to a chair. He still kept going on and on about pigs.

"Need to save the pig! Need to save the pig!"

"Yes, Dad, of course. Now why don't you come and sit down and have a nice cup of tea?"

Abby's mum steered her father to his chair, and she looked back and smiled weakly through her tear-stained eyes at Abby.

Abby couldn't cope; it was all too much. She turned and made her way out of the house and into the small garden. Pigeons were cooing, they seemed to be all around the garden. She could just about see Gloucester Cathedral, its majestic stone tower rising up through the houses. She had always noticed the great tower from a long way off whenever they were approaching the city. She turned and looked back towards the house and could see her mum's back in the window.

At that moment there was a great cacophony of sound which startled her. As the cathedral's majestic bells started their echoing, clanging routine, Abby started to totter; she lost her balance, she swayed and then tumbled over. She thudded violently onto the ground and she saw stars.

*

As she came to, she felt groggy, but was aware that the peal of bells was still chiming away; she was really disoriented, and she opened her eyes and looked around. She felt strange and she couldn't recognise her grandparents' garden; everything now seemed so different. Something was wrong, what had happened? The building had changed; it was timber-framed and had a thatched roof. The garden had no flowers. She was aware of a very unpleasant strong pungent smell.

"What's going on, where has everyone gone… Mum? Gran? Where are you? I don't like this."

When she was anxious, she would fiddle with her

hair. Now her fingers felt for her hair it felt so different, it seemed to be all greasy and straggly and something was on top of it. It was a bonnet of some sort. Her clothes felt all prickly and scratchy. She looked down. "What on earth is this?"

She saw that her clothes were different, dirty and like something from the olden days – she was now wearing some sort of tunic.

She was totally baffled. Was this some sort of awful joke being played on her?

"What is happening to me? This is unreal, my clothes, the houses and the stink all around. I only stumbled, didn't I? Come on, please, stop messing around! How can my clothes and everywhere change so quickly? What's going on? Am I turning out like poor old Grampy and being all mixed up?"

She now heard an ominous whistling sound passing overhead and she instinctively ducked down with her hands over her head. There was an almighty crashing, ripping sound, a splintering of wood nearby. She looked in the direction where the sound came from and she could see smoke billowing up. There were shouts and ear-splitting screams. She was frightened, she was trembling all over and her ears hurt with a horrible buzzing and ringing sound. There was now an awful acrid burning smell everywhere.

"What's happening, what's going on?"

A strong Gloucester accent asked, "Are you all right, Abigail?"

She turned to look in the direction of the voice. She saw a grubby boy peering at her. His clothes looked unusual; he had a sort of smock over tattered trousers and he was barefooted. He smiled a toothy grin at her.

"That be a real close one, reckons that will be it for today, just to keep us on our toes!"

Abby was bemused.

"What was that?"

"One of the King's balls. Stupid!"

"The King's balls? What on earth do you mean, King's balls?"

"Oh come on, Abigail, you know the King's men, they fire at least two or three cannonballs at us every day. Anyway, come on, we needs to find some food, I'm starving."

The boy ducked down and disappeared through a dingy passageway by the nearest house. Abby hesitated; she wasn't sure what to do.

"What is this? Mum! Where are you? I don't like this!"

The boy's voice called, "Come on, Abigail!"

She looked all around, hesitated, and then decided to follow him along the narrow passageway. She now saw more and more people in old-fashioned clothes and then two men who appeared to be soldiers from another world; they were carrying muskets. Were they real?

Abby was now struck by a thought. *Perhaps I've ended up in one of those things where everyone dresses up and pretends, now what are they called? Yes, that's it, a re-enactment! How has this happened? Maybe I just stumbled into it when the bells sounded. Weird!*

Now she could see people being helped from a smoking ruin. She was closer to those awful screams and then she saw the legs of a shattered body under a collapsed wall. She shuddered; this was no re-enactment! This was for real!

She exclaimed, "Where on earth am I?"

"You silly fool, Abigail, stop messing 'bout. Youse acting all funny like. Come on, I've got an idea to get us sum food, I need sumthing, ain't eaten for ages!"

He led her to where a great stone wall blocked their way.

"Now listen, Abigail, when we's get to Southgate and we tells them that we's need to go an' collect some driftwood from the river and I'll say I can get sum birds' eggs, 'cos we ain't got no food at home. They'll let us out because we're only young 'uns, but my plan is to go to the King's camp and see if we's can scrounge sum food or maybe nick sum."

Abby didn't know what to say; this all sounded a bit dangerous and she wondered how this boy knew her. She even wondered why he called her Abigail; only her mum called her that and that wasn't often – only usually when she had done something wrong. She started to think it was her overactive imagination working overtime again. First she had heard talking pigs, and now this! Was she in some sort of weird dream?

She hesitated and then blurted out, "King?"

"Charlie boy!"

She was puzzled; surely Prince Charles wasn't the king yet, was he? She just blurted out, "The King is here?"

"What's up with you? He's been outside the city since early this month and he wants it, don't he!"

"What? What does he want?"

"The city, Gloucester of course! Stop being stupid!"

Abby was totally lost, not only about where she was but also about what on earth was going on!

She could now see many more soldiers as they approached the gate. She looked carefully at one. He was dressed in a yellowish short coat with leather straps coming from each shoulder crossing over his chest. He wore strange-looking trousers and a sword dangled from his belt. On his head he had an armoured helmet with a great flap at the back and three bars at the front. There were other soldiers near the gate who didn't have swords but were holding great tall wooden spears. The main gate was shut, but there was a smaller gate next to it in the wall.

One of the soldiers spoke harshly at them. "Oi, where do you think you are going?"

The boy looked at the soldier and put on a pleading voice.

"Please, sir, we need more wood, can we just slip out quietly down to the river and collect sum?"

"Orders are orders – the gate stays shut! Them Royalists are so close, a real tricky lot as well. They are supposed be digging tunnels for mines, ain't they?"

"Oh go on, let us out – we ain't going to be any trouble for anyone. Might try for sum eggs while we're there, I'll bring one for you, promise! They ain't going to take any notice of us, 're they. We're not important, just a couple of young 'uns. Just think of a real fresh egg to eat. If we're lucky we might find a few."

The soldier's face creased with a smile. "Well, don't suppose two little ones will be a threat to them, but it is dangerous, don't trust anyone. Knock five times at the gate and the password for today when you come back is *Fairfax Fights for Freedom*! Don't tell that to anyone! Don't forget I want at least one egg and you be careful out there and don't tell anyone it was me who let you out!"

He pulled a grille back so he could peer out. "All clear, now go."

He pulled back a great bar and opened the gate a little way; the boy nipped through, quickly followed by Abby. Abby certainly couldn't believe what she now saw in the twilight. In the distance there were tents, with flags flying and lots of columns of smoke drifting up; she could see fires twinkling between the tents. She could make out the big river to her right; it looked so different to what she remembered.

The boy spoke in a quiet whisper.

"Come on! Make sure you duck down; we don't want to be an easy pot shot for anyone. We need to get down close to the river."

At that moment Abby felt her stomach gripped by butterflies and a nasty shiver ran down her spine. She now seemed to appreciate that this was for real. It was no game! Danger was lurking!

They ran low till they reached the river. The ground was damp and soft. The boy came to a halt.

He hissed at her, "Down!"

They threw themselves onto the ground. Abby managed to get a glance of two figures up ahead. They kept absolutely still. A whiff of pipe smoke drifted towards them. They could hear footsteps. Abby was terrified; she was shaking with fear and didn't know what would happen next.

A voice with a distinctive London accent now broke the silence.

"It ain't going to be long now, they surely will surrender any time soon. They must be nearly out of food. I'm getting fed up with all this waiting around. Don't know why we don't attack and get it all over and done with!"

The second voice answered, "It won't be long now; it should be easy! They must have had enough by now and must almost be out of food. Come on, let's go back to camp."

The voices trailed away into the gloom.

"Phew, that was really close. Come on, let's get going and be quiet!"

Abby was petrified. She followed the disappearing boy's shape. They were close to the river; she could hear the faint gurgle of the water and a distant duck. The boy stopped abruptly.

"There, just down here, I know there's a nest. I'll distract the bird, you grab as many eggs as you can, but be quick, they can be nasty brutes."

Abby could now make out the shape of the nest with the goose sitting on it. It hissed up at the boy and left the nest to see the boy off; Abby quickly reached down and snatched two eggs. The pair of them scrambled up the bank with their eggs. The goose started honking loudly. Another goose joined in and there was now an almighty din.

"Oh, darn it. Stupid old goose. Come on, quick now

– the guards will now be alert and on the lookout. Keep down."

There was a sharp bang and the air whistled threateningly as a musket ball flew past high above them.

"That's just a warning shot but we's need to be careful."

Abby was aware her heart was thumping and racing. She thought to herself, *What an earth has happened to me? This is some sort of weird nightmare, surely. I need to wake up. Come on, Abby, wake up!*

Instead, she stumbled and fell. The pain was real as her knee crashed into something.

"Abigail, you all right?"

She winced with pain from her knee.

"I think so!"

"Come on, quick!"

They could hear angry shouts of alarm coming from where the camp was. Abby was now limping, but they were going as fast as they could. It was obvious that in the camp the soldiers were now on full alert and were out looking for intruders.

"Down here!"

The boy ducked down into some reeds and Abby followed. They were both out of breath. He held a

finger to his mouth. The muddy ground was cold. The voices were now much closer; they could hear bushes and reeds being flattened with something. It was getting closer and closer, till the searchers were almost upon them. The reeds were pulled back and revealed a bearded face with a broad-brimmed hat with large colourful feathers popping out from the back. He pointed his musket at them. Abby was frozen rigid with fear.

Chapter 4

Over France
(May 1944)

"Target up ahead! All ready, Bomb Aimer?"

"Bomb doors open."

"Mid gun, check above that no one has their doors open directly above us. It would be just our luck to get hit by one of our own bombs!"

Tom looked up; he could see a Lancaster up above on the starboard side with its doors open.

"One up on our starboard side, Skip, about to unload!"

"Good, we will keep to our course. Aimer, are you ready?"

"Ready, Skip, hold your course. Straight ahead, almost there, steady, steady!"

Tom kept his eyes carefully on the Lancaster up on

the starboard side. A snowstorm of flak was filling the sky. He saw bombs tumbling down in deadly clusters from the other planes. He could see down below that there were black explosions all around the railway yards.

"Bombs away, hold your position, Skip! Need to take the dratted photo, steady, steady… OK all done. Take the old girl away, Skip!"

"Port, climb, port, climb again. Up, up and away we go!"

The sudden twists and steep climb made Tom's stomach churn. He felt bile rising up in his throat and swallowed uncomfortably. Despite the bitter freezing cold in the turret, he felt warm. He now could see a dark sinister shape moving quickly on the starboard side. He spoke into his intercom.

"Bandit starboard side, Skip!"

"Corkscrew, port, climb, port, climb."

The whole plane creaked as it climbed and zigzagged quickly.

Corkscrew was the command that evasive action was being taken. Luckily the night fighter didn't change course. Tom gripped his guns, anticipating the attack from the fighter. He was surprised to see the enemy aircraft now beginning to disappear as they continued their twisting path.

"Well done, Skip, he hasn't changed course!"

The flak was persisting, and the plane continued to be buffeted by the explosions all around. Tom winced when he saw another plane burst into flames and disintegrate.

"C for Charlie has bought it, Skip!"

"Let's just get out of here in one piece!"

Tom was now aware of the serpent-like hiss from his oxygen mask in the pause between the bursting shells exploding nearby.

"Keep those eyes peeled, boys; Mid gun, OK up there?"

"OK, Skip!"

As they gradually got further from the target the flak began to ease and the Lancaster's navigator was now guiding them away and home.

Chapter 5

Your Majesty!

"Well, well, well, what have we got here? Up! Hands in the air! They must be so desperate in the city, sending out children to spy on us!"

"Let's take them to Rupert now he is back. He will question them and then they will be dispatched."

Other soldiers had surrounded them, and the children were roughly handled. Abby didn't like the sound of the word 'dispatched' and she was terrified. The boy seemed unconcerned and looked relaxed.

She looked at him as they were being pushed and pulled towards the camp.

"What's going to happen to us?"

"We're going to be…"

A hand hit the boy hard on his back and a harsh voice snapped, "Quiet!"

As they stumbled into the tented camp, there was an unpleasant mix of pungent smells from the latrines and wood smoke. Abby saw there were many clusters of fires and tents. Stacks of muskets were balanced upright outside the tents. Soldiers were everywhere. They were pushed on, deeper and deeper into the camp. In front of them there were two much larger tents, both guarded by sentries with muskets resting on their shoulders.

A challenge rang out.

"Halt! Who goes there?"

"Rifleman Moore with two prisoners to see His Highness!"

"Pass, friend."

They were bundled roughly by their captor into the large tent.

Candles illuminated the tent. There were expensive-looking chairs and a large table with a map spread across it; sitting looking at the map was a youngish-looking man with flowing black hair, wearing a smart blue coat. He looked up quizzically at them.

"Vhat have we here – a young fraulein and boy. Vhy have you brought them to me?"

His foreign tone was harsh.

"My lord, we found these two lurking down by the river."

"Zhere must be spies, zhey must be struggling if zhey send out children to do zheir dirty jobs!"

The boy spat out, "We ain't no spies, we just wanted sumthing to eat, tried to get sum eggs from the river, that's all!"

"You expect us to believe that? You know what happens to spies! Vhat are your names?"

"Ain't no spy, just hungry! I'm John Ryan and she's Abigail Brown, both of Gloucester city."

"Vell I don't believe you. You will be taken away and shot!"

Abby felt her knees wobble and tears began to trickle down her cheeks.

At that moment there was a commotion outside the tent and suddenly two guards entered, followed by an important-looking, neatly bearded man wearing a black tall hat; he held a silver cane in his left hand to help him balance. He wore a blue sash, and it was fixed with a large type of rosette. There was a hush and quickly everyone dropped to one knee and bowed their head. John pulled a surprised Abby down, so they were like everyone else, on their knees.

The man spoke with a voice that had a gentle Scottish accent to it.

"Prince Rupert, what strange company you keep,

who are these children?"

Rupert replied, "Your Majesty, we have just apprehended these parliamentarian spies near your camp."

"Spies? But they are mere children!"

"Zhey are so desperate, zhey think children will not be taken seriously by us; but if we hadn't caught them zhey would have reported back our strength to Colonel Massey in the city. I was just about to have zhem shot as spies!"

Abby gasped and her whole body trembled. She was terrified and she started to sob.

John gripped Abby's arm and addressed the King.

"Your Majesty we's woz hungry! All we wanted woz sum eggs to eat. Look!"

He held out one of the eggs in his grubby hand.

The King looked carefully at them both. His eyes looked tired. He now smiled kindly in their direction.

"They are hungry, Rupert. So, is there no food in Gloucester? Otherwise, these children wouldn't be here, would they?"

Rupert answered, "So now, Your Majesty, is the time to attack. Zhey are out of food. Let us press home our advantage! Zhey won't have the strength to fight us. It vill be over quickly!"

The King shook his head gently.

"Yes, but if we storm the city many more people will be killed. If we wait a little longer until they have nothing left at all they will have to surrender. That way we will avoid unnecessary bloodshed."

"But your Majesty, if ve vait too long, Parliament might get reinforcements here. Ve have reports that Essex has an army moving this vay! Ve must strike now before he gets here!"

There was a pause; the King looked thoughtfully at Abby and John.

"Tell me, children, is that right, there is no food in Gloucester?"

Abby looked plaintively at John. He looked at the King. Abby could tell his brain was racing and thinking of what to say and then he spoke.

"Your Majesty, there is food in the city but it ain't for the likes of us. It's all for the soldiers so they can fight you. It is all guarded so that's why we need to find food for us otherwise we'll starve."

"The soldiers have food?"

John nodded. "Yes, Your Majesty."

The King turned to one of the guards. "Get them some bread and meat to eat. We are not fighting children!"

He then looked at Rupert. "I think we can use this moment to our advantage; these children can help us. We will let them go back to the city."

Rupert's eyebrows shot upwards. "I don't understand, Your Majesty?"

"The children can go back to the city. I think this young man is being loyal to his city. There won't be just food for the soldiers. He is making that up. That is a commendable quality, he is a brave young man."

"I still don't see vhy ve should let the children go. Zhey are spies, ve can't afford to let them go back to report on vhat zhey have seen!"

Abby decided she didn't like this Prince Rupert at all! Although he looked handsome and dashing, he was an unpleasant, uncompromising man who obviously didn't think twice about killing children.

The King raised his cane and tapped the table firmly.

"We are not making war on children! Our argument is with Parliament! I said, I think we can use these children to our advantage."

Rupert was not convinced.

"If ve let zhem go back zhey will be able to give reports on our strength – especially our guns."

"I think that with a spyglass from the walls they can easily see our numbers and our guns."

At that moment the rain started hammering on the tent.

"Your Majesty, zhey probably have seen the great cannon over on the priory, zhey may have seen the men starting to dig the tunnel towards Eastgate. But zheese children will be able to tell zhem about zhat in detail! It will harm our cause if zhey go back and report. Massey has repeatedly chosen his moments to attack us before!"

The rain outside was unrelenting.

The King looked at John and Abby. He now whispered to Rupert, "I'm sure Colonel Massey knows all about the great cannon and I don't think there will be much he can do about the tunnel, although this cursed rain is holding the digging up. Make sure we double the guard!"

Even though he was whispering Abby could hear every word. She still wasn't sure what was happening. Had she ended up in a film? But then there would have to be cameras everywhere, wouldn't there? As she looked around, she was convinced she had ended up at a moment in time sometime in the past, although she had no idea of when. She knew a lot about the Victorians from a school project, but who on earth was this King and who was this unpleasant Prince Rupert? She felt something touch her hand, it was John; she looked at him and he winked at her.

The King was still talking.

"No, I think these children can go back into Gloucester and they can tell Colonel Massey about how much food we have and what powerful weapons are at our disposal. They will then know their position is hopeless and they will have to press for terms. That way it will avoid unnecessary bloodshed and then we will have the city."

"I don't vant to go against your orders, Your Majesty, but—"

He stopped as a servant came in with food for the children. The King gestured for them to eat. John grabbed the bread and started to stuff it into his mouth, Abby took a chicken leg and started to gnaw at it. She actually felt incredibly hungry. John was also gobbling down the food as fast as he could.

"You see, Rupert, these children are hungry. I think the time is near, but I want to be sure and then we can press for the city's surrender. I have an idea of how we can achieve this."

They carried on in whispers, although the children could hear every word. The King continued, "Their morale will further weaken; it will stir up the people and foment dissent. Colonel Massey will then be told by the people to sue for surrender to us."

"I still zhink it is the time to attack if zhey are zhat veak!"

"I think we will send a spy later tonight to assess what strength they have. Then we will decide if it is the time to attack but I want to avoid unnecessary deaths if I can."

"Majesty…"

The King now turned and spoke to the children. "I am a just king, so you may have safe passage back to Gloucester and you can tell the people and Colonel Massey that their king is merciful; lives can be spared if the people of Gloucester open their gates and lay down their arms. This is important. I will write a letter to Colonel Massey for you to deliver."

The King moved to the table, picked up some parchment and a quill. He dipped the quill in an inkpot and started to write. When he had finished, he took hot wax from a pot and dripped it on the letter to seal it closed. He then stamped it with the royal seal.

Abby was watching, fascinated by this old-fashioned writing process.

"Here, take this to Colonel Massey. It is important! Lives depend on you. Do you understand?"

John wiped his mouth quickly and bowed his head towards the King.

"Yes I do, Your Majesty, and thank you."

He turned to Abby and grabbed her arm.

"Rupert, you will make sure these children are given safe passage back to the city."

"Majesty."

He led the children out of the tent and gave orders to two men to escort the children back to the city's south gate. It was now dark and wet, so the journey was difficult, and the men were cautious.

"We don't want to be a target for a pot shot so make sure you are quiet!"

"The rain will keep them from looking too hard and they won't want their powder to get wet!"

They tentatively made their way towards the looming dark walls. Their escorts whispered harshly, "Wait here till we are safely out of the way and then you can chance your luck and hope someone doesn't take a shot at you!"

With that they melted back into the darkness.

John led the way carefully back. As they got closer to the gate a voice shouted at them, "Halt, who goes there; friend or foe?"

"Friend! John Ryan and Abigail Brown… oh yes, *Fairfax Fights for Freedom*."

The grille of the door scraped open and a face peered at them.

"Enter."

Chapter 6

A Plan is Hatched

The door opened and they slipped through quickly, the door slamming behind them.

Torches flickered and flamed in the wall near them and two soldiers holding long pikes stood looking at them. One of them lowered his pike and pointed it at them. He spoke harshly at them.

"Well, well, what are you two doing out at night? What were you up to? No good, I bet! How do we know that you aren't Royalists come here to make trouble? Well, speak! What have you been up to out there?"

Abby gulped; she hadn't expected this. However, John wasn't at all troubled.

"Oi, don't be so stupid! We's went out looking for wood and eggs, but we's got taken. We saw the King and we's have a message from 'im to Colonel Massey."

"Likely story and pigs might fly!"

"Look at this you great lump!"

He pulled out the letter – he knew the men wouldn't be able to read but he wanted to be sure they could see the royal seal.

The man who had spoken and pointed the pike at them sneered.

"Is this some sort of trick? Why would the King give a letter to you two scraps?"

The other soldier put his hand on his companion's shoulder.

"Bert, that looks real! I think we should take them to the Colonel. We don't want to get into any trouble now, come on!"

"All right, but no funny stuff, you two!"

He raised his pike, holding it in one hand, and pushed John roughly with the other and the two of them were led along a major street and then turned left at a crossroads. Abby could make out the unmistakable and distinctive dark shape of the cathedral in the gloom on their right. At last, they came to what looked like an old-fashioned pub to Abby; it seemed vaguely familiar and was guarded by soldiers.

Some words were exchanged, and they stood for a while outside the building.

A soldier then came out and they were hustled inside. There was an imposing oak table with a map laid out on it, and sitting by it was a youngish man with shoulder-length black hair, moustached, with a small, pointed beard and a prominent nose. He was wearing a breastplate over a yellow tunic. He looked inquisitively up at Abby and John standing there with their two guards.

"Well, you two, I hear you have been wondering all over the countryside. Supposed to have spoken to the King as well! You two have got something for me? Is that right?"

Abby recognised a northern accent in the voice.

John blurted out, "Colonel Massey, sir, we woz just searching for eggs and we woz captured and we woz taken before Prince Rupert, he was going to have us 'ung or shot, we's didn't like him he weren't nice! We woz frightened but luckily the King came in and the King was cross with Rupert and he gave us sum food – we's had some real meat – and he said we had to come an' see you and tell you to surrender the city. He said to give you this letter. That's all! We's don't want no trouble, sir! Honest!"

The Colonel smiled.

"Slow down, John Ryan. So, you saw the King? You had better give me his letter."

John handed it over and Colonel Massey read it carefully.

"Well, this is to be expected, calling on us to surrender. Have you anything else to say? What about you, young lady? Your friend has done all the talking so far."

Abby blushed and spoke. "One thing I heard, when they were whispering so they thought we couldn't hear but I did hear, was about a big gun and tunnels, but they thought you knew that already. They were going to send a spy up to the walls tonight to see if they could work out how much food and stuff is left in the city. If they think there's no food and you don't surrender, then they will attack!"

Massey looked her up and down carefully. His staring eyes made her feel uncomfortable.

"You are really a first-class spy, Abigail Brown!"

"Only telling you what I heard."

"So, a spy is coming up to the city walls tonight?"

He paused and Abby could tell his brain was whirring away. Nobody moved or spoke.

At last, he grinned broadly.

"Perhaps we can give him something to think about! Yes, let's make him think! Sergeant Jones!"

"Sir?"

"I know food stocks are depleted. How many porkers are there left in the city? I know we are getting low."

"Sir, just the one left now. Old George!"

Massey frowned. "Oh dear! Only one pig, that won't do!"

"I'm sorry, sir."

John suddenly blurted out, "I knows what to do. You has to fool 'em! The spy can't see through walls, so he can only 'ear things! So what's you do is you get that pig near the wall and when that there spy comes up close you squeeze the pig real hard till it squeals. They're noisy so-and-sos; so the spy hears it on the other side! Then if the spy man moves somewhere else, youse move the pig near to where he goes and squeeze him again! Pig squeals again. So he thinks we have loads of pigs!"

"What? Ah ha! Yes, so he thinks we have plenty of pigs! John Ryan, you are brilliant; you could go far!"

John beamed with pride.

"Sergeant Jones, you've got the idea; have two men keep the pig close to the wall near Southgate. The men on guard will need to keep a low profile but keep a keen watch and they will signal down as soon as they see any movement outside. I should think it will be either Southgate or Westgate so be ready to move. No shouts, we must be quiet. Then, Sergeant Jones, you squeeze Old George hard till he makes a fuss – do you understand?"

John asked, "Can we watch? We's won't get in the way."

Massey looked at the children, he shook his head.

"You will only get in the way. No, you must go home now!"

The children found themselves outside the headquarters in the dark, where only a few torches blazed a smoky light.

"Abby, I'm just going home but I want to watch this. I've still got one egg that no one took from me and it ain't broke at all like the other one! So I'm going to get it home first. Meet you near Southgate in a bit."

Abby was about to ask where Southgate was, but John had already scampered away. She walked away from the soldiers on guard. Just at that moment the cathedral bells started their ringing. She felt dizzy again and her body started to sway. Then it all went blank.

Chapter 7

Bail Out

(May 1944)

They couldn't relax. There were sure to be other hazards to navigate before they got home.

"Twenty minutes to the coast, Skip!"

Tom, sitting up in his freezing turret, was beginning to relax; he was thinking about the welcoming steaming mug of tea and hearty breakfast that would be waiting back in the mess.

Suddenly the plane jolted as it was unexpectedly ripped by a volley of cannon shells. Sparks flew and the port wing burst into flames. Tom watched with horror as the flames started to creep along the wing.

"Fire, port wing!"

"Hang on chaps, let's see if we can put it out with some jiggery pokery!"

The skipper dipped the port wing and then dived steeply down to see if his actions would put out the fire. Tom could see the flames licking their way towards the fuselage.

"Flames still coming, Skip!"

"One last go to see if we can put it out, chaps! Hang on again!"

He repeated the manoeuvre but with no success. He tried weaving from side to side. All of them were gripped with tension, praying for the flames to be extinguished.

"No good chaps, just going to drop our altitude."

The plane descended. Flak once more was bursting all around.

"Abracadabra! Bail out! Abracadabra! Bail out! I'll keep her steady while you all get out!"

The plane creaked and groaned with pain. Tom awkwardly managed to squeeze himself out of the turret; he picked up his chute. He looked back along the fuselage to where the rear gunner, Fred, was; he was looking back at him. Tom now pointed to his own parachute and Fred knew what that meant and put his thumb up. Tom managed to clip on his parachute as quickly as he could. He got to the door and pulled it open. The air rushed past, the acrid smell of burning filled his nostrils. He could see clouds of flak bursting

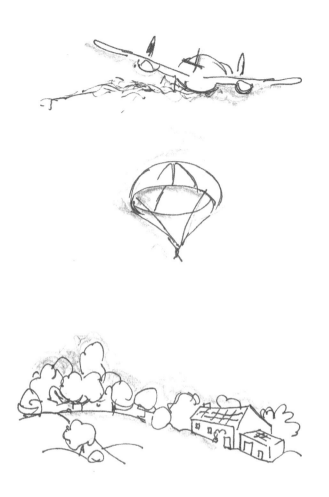

across the sky. He paused for a split second and then leapt out into the darkness. His breath was taken away by the rushing air; he pulled the cord and was yanked upwards. He was floating, he was cold, and he felt all alone. He hoped everyone had got out. Now he was shaken by a great explosion. Tom flinched: was that his plane? He continued to drift down, his mind racing: what should he do? He remembered one part of his training.

"Hide your parachute, try not to leave any clues."

Thud!

Pain raced up his body, all the air seemed to be sucked out of him. He tumbled over and over. He managed to stagger to his feet, but as the parachute filled with the night breeze it pulled him over again. Once again, he struggled to his feet, unclipping his harness. He pulled at the straps and now fought hard to control his recalcitrant chute. He steadily gathered in the material, wrapping it into the smallest bundle possible and now hugged it protectively to his stomach. He could just make out some trees nearby; it looked like the edge of a wood or forest. He made his ungainly way towards the trees. He knew he needed to get really well under the cover of the trees because no doubt search parties would be sent out. He tripped and staggered into a thicket of bushes that tore at his clothes. He realised that this would be an ideal place for hiding his parachute. He pulled back the branches and then pulled out the knife he carried, then he dug into the soil as quickly as he could. Before long he had managed to semi-bury the chute and cover the top with branches and leaves. He now moved on deeper and deeper into the safety of the trees before it got light.

Chapter 8

The Clues Are in the Past!

"Abby, Abby, are you all right? You look miles away."

"What? Where?"

Abby found herself standing in her grandparents' garden with those familiar pigeons cooing all around her.

"Abby? I just asked if you wanted a cup of tea. Didn't you hear me?"

"Mum? But, but…?"

She didn't know what had happened; it was all so worrying.

"You look as if you are in another world! You seemed to be miles away."

Her mother paused for a moment.

"Look, Abby, I know this is upsetting for us all, but we will get through this, I hope. We just need to support each other and stay positive. We just need to get some help."

Abby was totally bewildered. She looked down at her clothes; they were her normal clothes again – not rough and old.

"Mum, how long have I been here?"

"Pardon? What do you mean, how many times we have been in this garden? You first came here as a baby."

"No, how long have I been out in the garden?"

"Abby, are you playing games or something? We have only just got to Gloucester; you said hello to your grandparents and then you came out here! Look, I don't want any silly stuff at the moment; I think we have enough going on, don't you?"

Abby looked all around and at her mum. The garden was as she had always remembered it, the old apple tree was in the corner; small early apples were festooned all over it. She had no idea what on earth was going on. It must have been a dream, surely? It had seemed so real and it had felt like hours since those bells had sent her tumbling. Yet her mum said that she had only been out in the garden for a few minutes. How could she make up all those people and stuff? She didn't think she could say anything about it now; she didn't want to give her mum even more to worry about, even though she herself was confused and worried!

"Sorry, Mum, I'm just a bit muddled about things…"

Her mum smiled; her eyes were wet, and she moved to her and enveloped her with her arms.

"Oh, come on, love, I could do with a hug."

They both stood there for a moment and the pigeons serenaded them with cooing.

"Let's go and have tea with Granny and Grandad."

As they moved back to the house Abby was surprised and alarmed to feel an aching pain in her knee that hadn't been there before!

Later, while her grandad was dozing peacefully in his favourite old battered and worn chair and her mum was helping her gran in the kitchen to prepare supper, Abby started to use her phone to look up things. She googled 'King Charles'. She read, 'King Charles 1st was king of England from 1625 till he was executed in 1649'. Her eyes were scanning through the information; she discovered he was a Stuart. She had heard of them – she knew they came after the Tudors! The bit that got her really interested was when she read that he had had a quarrel with parliament.

Her mum came into the room. Careful not to wake her father, she asked Abby in a whisper, "You're not playing games on that phone, are you, Abby? You know I don't want you to spend too much time looking at a screen. It's not healthy."

Abby was affronted and whispered back, "Actually, I was reading about King Charles and his argument with parliament."

"Really? Why on earth are you doing that? Is it something you have to do for school in the holiday?"

"No, just wanted to know about it. I thought I should know something about Gloucester as we are here."

"Well, you know a lot happened here in Gloucester; there was a siege for a few weeks during the Civil War. Dad – Grampy – used to know all about what happened; he often used to go on and on about it when your uncle and I were kids. I remember he used to give talks about it locally."

Her mum pointed to the bookshelf behind Abby.

"He has got quite a few books and pamphlets all about it up there on the shelf. Apparently, the King was camped only a couple of miles from where we are standing now!"

Abby felt a cold shiver run down her back and she swivelled round and looked up at the shelf. She had never really taken any notice of the books at her grandparents'; she never thought they were for her and they seemed so old-fashioned to look at. She noticed one entitled *The Siege of Gloucester*; she reached up and pulled the book out. This was all getting difficult; why had she suddenly dreamt about something that had happened nearly four hundred years ago? Perhaps she had met some ghosts from that time – but she didn't believe in that sort of stuff, did she? Maybe it was this book that had triggered her 'dream', but she hadn't ever looked at it before, well, at least, she didn't think so.

"Supper will be ready soon, but we will wait till your grandfather wakes up. It's good for him that he's so peaceful."

Abby nodded and sat back down with the book. She flicked through the pages, looking at the pictures. Some were old maps for the city showing where the armies had been, others were paintings of people. She gasped with surprise when she saw one picture of a handsome young soldier with a distinctive angular nose, flowing black hair and moustache and goatee-type beard. He was wearing a breastplate

over a yellow tunic. She didn't need to read the words underneath the picture; she knew who it was straight away.

"Colonel Massey!"

Her grandfather stirred in his chair and opened his eyes. He smiled benignly at her.

"Hello!"

"Hi, Grampy, did you have a good sleep?"

He carried on smiling.

"Hello!"

"I was looking at one of your books, Grampy."

"Hello!"

"I was reading one of your books, Grampy."

"Who are you?"

"It's me, Abby! Mum and I came especially to see you."

"Hello! Who are you?"

Abby patiently replied again, "It's Abby, your granddaughter."

Her grandfather pushed himself up from the chair; he wobbled unsteadily for a moment and shuffled over to Abby's chair. Abby looked at him anxiously but stayed seated, with the book open on Massey's picture, still resting on her lap. He reached down for the book and looked at the picture.

"Massey! Massey! Poor piggy! Poor piggy!"

"He's not a pig, Grampy, he's a soldier!"

"Poor piggy!"

Abby was relieved when her mum came in and came over to where they both were.

"Hello, Dad, did you have a good sleep? Are you surprised to see Abby looking at one of your special books? She will be careful with it. Supper's nearly ready – shall we go through so we can eat?"

Abby watched her mum lead her dad through to the dining area and then she looked down again at the picture of Colonel Massey.

"Well, Colonel Massey, I seem to have pigs wherever I am! Either back at Marie's farm, or in that weird dream with you or with my grandad going on and on about them all the time! Now I have even met you, although you died hundreds of years ago. I just can't escape from all of this!"

The meal was awkward because of Abby's grandfather, who kept wanting to get up and look out of the window. Abby's mum and grandma would gently and patiently get him back to the table. It was a relief later when eventually he was settled in his bed. Abby's mum and grandmother were sitting at the table discussing what to do. There was a bottle of red wine on the table and two glasses half-full of wine.

"Mum, he needs to be looked after now; and you are absolutely exhausted, you can't keep this up."

"This is our home; we have been married for fifty-two years and have never been apart. He loves looking at the birds and touching his books. This is his home."

"But he is so restless. Apart from sleeping in the chair he is always on the move. He isn't safe!"

Abby chipped in with her thoughts.

"That's because Gramps loves seeing animals; look how he keeps going on about pigs! He needs to be able to get outside and see things."

"Mum, won't you just let me go and have a look around at homes where he might be able to settle?"

At this moment Abby's grandmother started sobbing.

"It's so hard... I want to look after my George... Oh, Mel, I just don't know what's for the best."

Abby's mum moved over to hug her mother. She whispered to Abby, "Just go and have a look in on your grandfather; it will just give us a bit of time to talk together. I think you should think about going to bed yourself. I'll come and see you later. Don't worry, love."

Abby kissed them both and made her way up the stairs to her grandparents' room. She could hear her grandfather's steady rhythmical breathing and she smiled. She remembered what her grandfather used to say to her when she was little, so she whispered, "Night, night, sleep tight, don't let the bed bugs bite – or should that be sleep tight the pig will be all right!

"Why did I say that? I seem to be becoming so obsessed with pigs!"

She felt the need to go outside for some fresh air before she got ready for bed. As she slipped back down the stairs, she heard a snippet of her mum talking.

"It will be for the best and yes, we will make sure it is right."

Abby was soon in the garden enjoying the scents. A tawny owl hooted loudly from close by and startled Abby, so she shut her eyes for a moment to see if she could hear anything else.

She was surprised when she felt a gentle poke from behind. She opened her eyes again and looked around and there he was again – John Ryan! She was back in the dark Gloucester streets. She wasn't *really* surprised.

Chapter 9

The Hero of Gloucester

"You coming, Abigail, to see wot happens with this here spy and the pig?"

Abby nodded and John started to move quickly towards Southgate with Abby following behind. It wasn't long before they could see up ahead a group of soldiers below the city walls. There was a flaming torch fixed to the wall that illuminated the scene in what seemed to be a mix of ghostly flickers.

"Let's stay here and watch, we don't want to get into any more trouble."

They thought they could see the unmistakable shape of a pig in the middle of the soldiers. As their eyes adjusted to the strange light Abby could just about

make out the light body of the pig with black spots
dotted all over its body. She muttered, "Gloucester Old
Spot."

"Ssssshhhhhhh, Abby!"

She didn't say anything; they stayed in the shadows
and carried on watching. They could see there were
some men up on the parapet, crouched down, peering
over the top. Time seemed to stand still, and Abby found
her back was beginning to ache from standing so long.
At last, there was some movement on the parapet; one
of the soldiers beckoned for everyone to be quiet below.

Abby and John both felt tense, it was obvious something was happening out on the other side of the wall.

John now whispered to Abby, "I reckon they have seen that spy; he must be getting close to the wall. Let's see what happens now!"

The soldier who was crouching on the parapet now gave the signal, a wave. The soldiers down at the bottom of the wall moved forwards. One of them held the rope holding the pig tightly whilst his companion held a pair of tongs around the pig's waist and squeezed. An almighty terrible squeal filled the air; the pig started to struggle and carried on squealing loudly. Abby was shaken by the noise, it seemed to go right through her. The soldier on the wall now signalled to stop and pointed along the wall to his right. John whispered, "I reckon the spy has moved away. Look at the soldiers, they're moving with the pig."

The soldiers were dragging along the distressed pig and were now moving on in the direction where the soldier had just pointed. John and Abby followed at a discreet distance. Once more there were some soldiers crouching on the wall watching carefully through the parapet. The pig party came to a halt although the pig was pulling at the rope. Again, there was a 'keep quiet' signal from the soldier on the wall. Abby now spoke quietly, "The spy must be there again close to the wall."

Everyone was quiet, waiting for the signal. Once again, the whole action was repeated; a wave from the wall and the pig was squeezed by the tongs and those awful squeals filled the air.

John smiled.

"I think it's working; look, they're moving onto another part of the wall. Come on, we're fooling the King with this. This is good!"

Abby was reluctant to follow. She was uncomfortable seeing the distress the pig was going through but she didn't know what else to do, so she followed behind.

The whole thing was repeated once more and again everyone moved on.

The party once more stopped by the wall and waited; this time the pig had twisted round and, instead of being sideways on to John and Abby, his head was facing directly at them. The pig's face was lit surreally by a nearby flaming torch and it looked exhausted and pained. Abby felt it was now looking straight at her. She felt unsettled by the pig's unrelenting stare. She now could hear a strange almost faraway voice that was strangely familiar.

"Are you just going to stand there and watch? Can't you stop them?"

She looked around to see where the voice came from, but all she could see was the pig party, the man on the wall and John.

"John, did you say something just then?"

"Ssshhhh, Abigail – or we will get into trouble with the soldiers."

She whispered back, "I thought I heard someone talking to us just now."

"Just be quiet and watch!"

Abby was bemused, she was sure she had heard something. Then, there was no mistaking it, she heard the voice again; it now seemed to be struggling to breathe.

"This will be the end of me, please stop them, please."

The man on the wall moved and waved to the pig knot of soldiers below. The pig wriggled, twisted, and pulled on the end of the rope in an effort to escape the deadly tongs. There was no escape; the soldier brought the tongs down onto the pig's waistline and squeezed hard. Abby could see the pig's face racked with pain; its eyes now seemed to lock onto hers. The ear-splitting squeals were awful to hear. The animal was in agony; the squeals seemed to be saying, "Why, oh why?"

Again, and again.

The pig convulsed, twisted by the excruciating pain, and collapsed in a heap on the ground. The soldier who was holding the rope tugged and pulled hard, but the pig didn't move. The soldier now kicked at the prostrate pig. Abby couldn't stand this; she rushed from their hiding place across towards the soldiers.

"Leave him alone! Look at the poor thing!"

One of the soldiers now raised his musket in alarm but Abby was already by the pig.

John rushed after her and spoke to the soldier.

"She don't mean any 'arm, it woz us who told the Colonel about the spy coming to the walls. All we woz doing woz watching to see what happened."

The soldier in charge now spoke.

"You could have ruined our operation so who's to say you are not really Royalist spies? The Colonel needs to know what happened so come with me now!"

Abby was bent over the pig. She reached down and touched it. She knew straight away that the pig was dead.

"Poor thing is dead."

The soldier laughed.

"Well, at least we are going to have some fresh meat now! Come on, off to the Colonel!"

John took Abby's arm and gently pulled her away from the body of the pig.

"Come on, Abigail, we's better face the music and not get ourselves into any more trouble!"

The pair of them followed the soldier back through the dark street, past the great building of the cathedral, to Colonel Massey's headquarters in the Crown Inn. Abby was in deep thought, thinking about the poor old pig; it had reminded her of old Herbert back at Marie's farm and those words she thought he had said.

He was right about Gloucester being a dangerous place for pigs, or at least it certainly is for this poor pig in particular.

They were made to stand outside Colonel Massey's room whilst one of the soldiers went in. They heard murmurings behind the door. It then swung open and Massey strode out, glaring angrily at them both.

"Well, well, our two adventurers. What have you got to say? You could have ruined everything, and the city could have been lost!"

"Please, Mister Colonel sir, we's just wanted to see what happened and we kept out of the way but Abigail ain't been herself lately, so she got all funny about the pig when it died! Sorry, sir."

The Colonel looked thoughtfully at Abby.

"Well, young lady, what is all this fuss about a pig? They are a valuable resource, you know."

Abby paused for a moment and looked up at Colonel Massey.

"I just think it should have been treated with more respect; your man kicked it!"

"It is just a pig! An animal! We eat them!"

"Yes, but this *pig* may well have saved the city so it should be treated properly and deserves respect!"

Massey's eyes twinkled with mischief and he smiled at Abby.

"You are right; if our plan has worked and the King thinks we have plenty of pigs and food, he may well delay his final assault, although I'm sure Prince Rupert might have different ideas. If they delay, then maybe Essex's relief can get here. So yes, you could say that pig is the 'Hero of Gloucester' but I'm afraid it won't get a special funeral. It will be toasted by the men, when it is roasted, and they have full stomachs!"

Abby shivered at the thought.

"Be gone, you two! I don't want to see you again. Next time I may not be so merciful. Stay out of trouble!"

*

Meanwhile, back at the King's camp, the spy had returned and was reporting to King Charles in his tent. He bowed low in front of the King, who was sitting in a large beautifully carved oak chair. Prince Rupert and several other commanders were standing on both sides of the chair.

"Ah, Captain Pollard, pray what have you to report?"

Captain Pollard bowed.

"Majesty… I managed to make my way up to the walls unseen. I kept to the shadows, so I couldn't be seen, and I listened carefully. I could hear some soldiers moving about on the other side of the wall, so I was as quiet as possible. I managed to get close to three of the city walls. During my time near the walls, I could hear many pigs squealing all over the city; it was an awful noise that made your blood freeze. So alas, Your Majesty, I conclude that at this moment there does appear to be much food in the city."

The King sat impassively while his commanders debated what to do.

"That means they will be fit and strong at this moment. We may need to wait before we can attack."

"If we delay, Essex's army might get here, and we would certainly be outflanked!"

"If we should hit them with sustained artillery it will surely make them sue for terms."

Prince Rupert now spoke. "Your Majesty, I must implore you to attack now, otherwise their relief will get here. It will damage our cause significantly if ve delay; I suggest ve prepare for an assault tomorrow!"

The King looked around the tent at his officers. He cleared his throat.

"Erm, erm, I have said before I want to avoid unnecessary bloodshed and from what Captain Pollard has reported there is still much food in Gloucester. There appear to be many pigs there at the moment. If that is the case, they may well also have plenty of shot and gunpowder. They are likely to put up a strong and spirited defence. We know that Colonel Massey is a capable soldier; he has made it difficult for us already with his forays out to attack us. The weather is also against us with this cursed rain ruining our attempts to mine the walls. I think we should wait and continue the siege for longer… until their morale is completely broken. Essex won't be able to move his army that quickly, not with this weather!"

"But your Majesty…"

"My decision is final! Keep the men in position and send out scouts to find out where Essex's army is."

*

John and Abby had left Colonel Massey's Headquarters.

"Phew, we are out of trouble now, and Abby, don't you go and spoil it and go and be all silly about pigs anymore. Right! I've got to go home."

With that he disappeared off into the darkness.

Abby opened her mouth to say something but too late, as he was gone.

She stood there and wondered what she should do now. She looked around; she felt lost without John in this other world. She didn't really know where she was; the city was dark, with only a few torches burning giving some poor light. She didn't know the city at all well. She thought, if she got to the cathedral, she might be able to get some sort of idea of how to make her way to the area of the city where her grandparents lived. Just at that moment she heard the tawny owl hoot. She instinctively shut her eyes and held them tight. She stood there for some time; she felt her nose was being assaulted by a delightful mixture of the scent of flowers and then she opened her eyes. She wasn't surprised to find that she was back in her grandparents' garden. She heard the back door open. She turned and looked to see her mum come out.

"I thought you had gone up to bed?"

Abby paused for a moment and then answered, "A long story, Mum, but I thought some fresh air might help me sleep."

"Well, your grandmother and I have talked, and we have a difficult time ahead of us. Now we all need some sleep. Go off to bed now."

Chapter 10

Lost in France (May 1944)

Tom had made good ground since he had hidden his parachute, but he was exhausted, and his ankle was throbbing with pain from his landing. He needed to rest somewhere and be out of sight when it got really light, which wouldn't be that long now. He saw some bushes nearby and decided this was as good a place as any. He wriggled into the bushes and found there was a bit of a dip underneath so that he could curl up; he would try and catch some shut-eye and then he could think what action to take. He certainly didn't want to end up in a prisoner of war camp – and that is if he was lucky! He pulled up the zip of his flying jacket and tried to rest.

Then he heard a lorry engine grinding in the distance. As it got closer it slowed to a halt; he heard harsh voices shouting, dogs barking and then shrill whistles. He pressed himself down as flat as he could and kept still. He felt his pulse racing away; he was terrified of being discovered. The shouts and dogs' excited barks were becoming fainter and he was relieved that the soldiers were obviously moving away till the sounds were lost in the night.

Despite the agony and discomfort from his ankle he now began to relax and after some time even managed to doze fitfully. When he eventually came to, he was unsure how long he had been there. It was now light. Tom peered through the bushes at his surroundings. He was, as he had thought, deep in a forest and, apart from birds singing and the breeze flicking the branches of trees, all was quiet. He couldn't hear anything that indicated the presence of humans. He was aware that he was hungry; he regretted he was missing the welcome back breakfast at the airfield! He pulled out a bruised apple that he carried in his pocket and ate it ravenously. He was now sure that nobody was nearby so he gradually hauled himself out of the bushes. He tentatively moved away from his hiding place and explored his surroundings. He limped slowly through the wood, going from tree to tree, pausing to check all was clear. After ten minutes of creeping through the wood he could see that beyond the trees was open farmland. He carefully moved forwards, making sure he was covered by the trees to the very edge of the wood.

He could see a dilapidated farm building with damaged fences marking old animal pens outside. He wondered if he would be able find some food and maybe a way of contacting the Resistance for help. He wasn't sure how he would be able to do that when he couldn't even speak French. When he was sure there was no one around he crept up to the building. He worked his way along the edge as quietly as he could. He reached the corner and slowly peered around it to see if the coast was clear. Then he heard the unmistakable click of a rifle bolt being pulled back behind him. His whole body quaked with fear. There was no escape. He turned to see the barrel of the rifle pointing at his head.

Chapter 11

Touching Base

Abby's mum had been right; it *was* difficult. There were lots of phone calls made and visits to many homes. Abby spent time with her grandfather; he seemed happiest walking round the garden, touching the leaves on the trees and gazing at the birds.

She remembered how, when she was little, he would take her for long walks in the woods pointing out the flowers and naming the birds. Now he mainly nodded and smiled. He was especially fascinated watching the swallows that came swooping past.

One afternoon they were sitting on a bench watching the birds, while her mum and Granny were inside talking about the homes for him.

"That bird is called a swallow, Grampy!"

"They will be off soon. Going south! Going south, migration!"

Abby was surprised by this answer and thought she must tell her mother about it.

"Yes, maybe in four or five weeks they will be off."

She heard the door of the house open and her granny wandered out.

"You two all right out here?"

"Yes, we have been watching the birds, haven't we, Grampy?"

He smiled and nodded.

"I'll sit with George, now, you go and have some time for yourself. I'm sorry, Abby, this can't be much of a summer holiday for you."

Abby got up and went over to her gran and kissed her.

"It's fine. I've actually learnt a lot about Gloucester this time and I never really noticed the older buildings before. You could say that I'm sort of seeing them all differently now. There's a lot of history all around, isn't there?"

"There is, but they have ruined a lot of it, knocking down buildings and replacing them with awful concrete. These days they are trying hard now to look after what remains."

Abby left her gran and went into the house; her mum was sitting at the table staring at her laptop. She turned her head when she heard Abby.

"Hello, love, everything OK outside?"

"Yes, Gran is with Grampy. You know, when I told him the name of a swallow, he said, 'Going south,' and used the word migration! He does come out with things that surprise you."

"Yes, sometimes he seems to be all there, doesn't he? Then the next minute he is like a child. Having said that, Gran can't manage him on her own, especially when he goes wandering off. At least he is not aggressive – that can often happen. Gran and I can't find anything yet that we can agree on. We are going to one this afternoon. I think we will all have to go; Grampy, and you, Abby, so it won't be ideal."

"OK. I am going to phone Marie, see what life is like back home, if that is OK?"

Abby chatted away to Marie to find out what everyone was doing back at home; it didn't seem that much, as quite a few people were away on holiday. Despite everything that had happened to her since she had been in Gloucester, Abby was keen to know if anything had happened to Herbert (the old pig on Marie's farm).

"How is the farm, Marie? Anything much happened since I've been stuck here?"

Well, that started Marie off on how Kenny, her horse, was behaving.

"Well, the last couple of days he has been really funny – he has become ever so frisky. Dad has told me not to ride him for a while as it might be dangerous; oh yes, the sheep are taking no notice of the dogs and they are making life awkward for Dad. The geese keep pecking at you when you get near them. They really hurt me the day before yesterday. The chickens won't come out of their house. Dad says he has never known anything like it in all his years of farming."

Abby wanted to hear about Herbert, as Marie

seemed to have mentioned most of the other animals on the farm. So she interrupted, "What about Herbert? Is he still around?"

She felt anxious about what the reply might be and, although she knew it was daft, she instinctively crossed her fingers.

"Well, he was supposed to go off last Thursday, but first of all, Dad's Land Rover broke down and he had to spend all day sorting it out. Then the trailer had a flat tyre the next day. He had some other jobs to do, so by the time he was ready, and he finally phoned the abattoir to book Herbert in, they said they were closed for at least a fortnight. They are worried about some infection or something, so they are having to disinfect everything!"

"So Herbert is still with you then?"

"Yes, Dad says he is the luckiest pig around! He's got another fortnight at least because the abattoir will have such a backlog!"

Abby smiled and uncrossed her fingers. They carried on talking about other stuff and Marie asked, "How are things for you in Gloucester? How are you getting on with your grandad and everything?"

"Well, we are going somewhere to look at a home this afternoon. Mum is desperate to sort something out for him while we are here. I've been exploring Gloucester's history; it is really interesting!"

Marie chuckled.

"Are you feeling OK, Abby? History and you don't seem to go together!"

Abby laughed as well.

"Well, I've got to do something while I'm here, otherwise I will die of boredom because there is nothing else to do here!"

"Good luck this afternoon!"

Chapter 12

A Possible Solution?

Later they all were in the car driving out of the city in a southwards direction. Abby saw the sign for Llanthony Secunda Priory. She read the sign and suddenly a light bulb flashed in her head. She informed everyone in the car, "That's near where the King had his camp during the siege! I read about it. They fired a great big cannon from here at the city, but it toppled over."

"Wow! You have been busy, young lady!"

Her grandfather started to sing, "All the king's men and all the king's horses couldn't put Humpty together again!"

Abby turned round to look at her grandad in the back of the car and she laughed gently.

"Very good, Grampy; you know that cannon wasn't really Humpty Dumpty, but it is a good story!"

Her mum was also smiling as she drove.

"Oh, listen to our historian, Dad, you always used to tell me about the siege when I was Abby's age. So where did you find that out, Abby?"

"Oh, I just read about it in one of the books back at Grampy's."

"Well, there are lots of stories about that time and Gloucester is proud of its history now. It does seem like the King made a big mistake by not attacking and storming the city. At least that's what Dad always used to tell me. His Majesty shouldn't have hesitated."

"Well, he didn't want unnecessary bloodshed. He was a decent man in lots of ways, even if he wasn't that bright; he was arrogant and messed up, big time," said Abby.

"Sounds like you almost knew him the way you are talking."

Abby felt her face blush and she decided not to say anything else. Eventually Abby's mum turned the car into the nursing home car park. Abby looked all around her. The house was an old large, ramshackle Cotswold stone building that seemed to be from another world; Abby liked the look of it. As they got out of the car, they could hear clucking chickens and a braying donkey.

"Listen to that donkey, Dad."

"Eeh haw, eeh haw!"

A lady with a bright blue flowery top over her trousers met them with a cheery smile. She shook hands with them all as they introduced themselves and she spoke kindly to Abby's grandfather.

"Hello, George, I'm Alice! Would you like to see our garden? I hear you love gardens."

She took his hand and led him to a doorway. She stopped to type a code into the pad by the door and then led him into the garden area; everybody else followed.

"Please, Abby, will you make sure that door is shut properly behind; we have to make sure the garden is secure so no one can wander off."

As they entered the garden Abby gasped, as she was met by a wonderful kaleidoscope of colour. Borders with flowers and bushes interspersed with a variety of trees ran around a large rectangular garden; in the middle there was a mixture of grass and yet more trees with two more flower beds. Paths ran parallel to the borders and there were some seats and tables scattered haphazardly throughout. There were a few people walking, one or two were being supported by younger people and one person was being pushed in a wheelchair. A few chickens were strutting across the grass. Abby's eyes scanned all around; she looked towards the building and there was a large, glazed area with large glass doors open. The donkey's braying attracted their attention and Abby turned to the far end of the garden and she noticed there was a farm-like area. There were some stables, a pen with goats, a chicken run and what looked like a pigsty.

She looked across at her grandfather, who was smiling.

"What do you think, Grampy? There are lots of animals and there are loads of birds in the bushes and the trees."

"Where is piggy?"

Alice spoke gently, "Yes, we have goats, chickens, a donkey, a pony and some sheep but sadly we haven't got a pig at the moment."

"No piggy?"

"No George; sadly, our last pig is no longer with us."

She looked at Abby's mum.

"All the animals are given to us as gifts; they often need a home so hopefully one day a pig might turn up for us."

Abby's brain started to whirr into action. She looked at the empty pigsty and her grandfather standing looking into it. Marie's farm and old Herbert came into her mind.

Maybe that would be the answer. She wondered how much a pig cost; Herbert would be just right here!

They spent time looking all around the building, the rooms and the dining area. Her grandfather contentedly ambled off on his own, enjoying the delights of the garden, stopping to touch the leaves of the trees. Abby squeezed her granny's hand; she was watching him all the time and Abby nodded towards her disappearing grandfather.

"Granny, look at him; he is happy here. It is made for him!"

Her grandmother smiled and blew her nose as a tear trickled down her cheek.

"Yes, but he is my George…"

Abby's mother put her arm around her mother.

"Oh, Mum! It is lovely here. You know he will be safe here and there is a bus stop right outside; you can come here whenever you want. I'd be worried about you trying to cope at home on your own. You both have done so well over the last couple of years or so."

Abby threw her arms around her granny.

"Oh, Granny… I tell you what would really make it perfect for Grampy, is if there was a pig here. I think the place could do with a pig!"

Alice, who was still with them, laughed gently.

"Yes, it certainly could do with a pig, so if you know anyone who has one spare – we will have it!"

*

Later, when they got back home from their visit, Abby was strolling around the garden with her grandfather, while her mum and grandmother talked things over back in the house. He was watching a blackbird strutting around on the grass.

"He is funny, he thinks he owns the place… Did you like the home we visited, Grampy?"

Her grandfather laughed at her and was surprisingly lucid.

"Yes… lovely garden with birds, but it needs a pig!"

"Yes, I agree, Grampy, it does need a proper pig!"

She laughed.

"Just leave it to me, Grampy. I've got an idea, but I need to work on it."

*

Later when she was clearing away the supper plates with her mum, Abby asked, "Mum, that was just right, that place for Grampy, wasn't it?"

"Yes, and I think Granny Sue is gradually coming round to it."

"When will he go there if Granny says it is OK?"

"Well, we are lucky there is a space, so I am hoping possibly in the next fortnight or so. Just a few things to sort out. We are popping home tomorrow and we can do the things that need doing on the phone, so we will have a week or so at home and then we will come back here to help Granny Sue. I've organised some help to come in until then. We are lucky that my dad has some savings to help pay for this; lots of people aren't so lucky these days."

Abby thought to herself about all this to-ing and fro-ing, she knew she would be going to her dad's for the latter part of the holiday. *That seems like a big chunk of the holiday already taken care of! Not sure where my stuff comes into all this. Perhaps I should do something when I get home and make the most of it!*

*

There were quite a few tears when they set off for home. Abby's mum and gran held each other in a tight embrace, while Abby held her grampy's hand; although he was smiling, he seemed to be lost in another world.

"Now don't worry, Mum, we will be back next weekend, and someone will call in every day. You must try and give yourself a break, otherwise you won't be able to keep going."

"I know, but I'm still not sure about all this. I'm sure we could manage here."

"Oh, come on, Mum, you can't watch him all the time, and that place was just right for Dad! You saw how happy he was there!"

Eventually goodbyes were said.

As Abby opened the car door her grandfather spoke.

"Needs Piggy! He must be saved!"

Abby gulped. She couldn't work out if through all that Alzheimer's stuff he knew something. Was that about the poor pig way back from the time of the siege? Or did he mean Herbert? Had she said anything about Herbert to him? She didn't think so. She knew that this was all ridiculous, but it was nagging her as she waved goodbye. *What does he know? Or is it just the way he says things?*

Abby's mum, whose eyes were red, spoke as soon as they were out of sight.

"You mustn't worry too much, Abby. It is going to be difficult for all of us. I'm sorry you have to see all this. I think once we get Grampy settled at that home it will be better all round, although not necessarily any easier for us all to bear."

Abby now asked her mum a question. "Mum, do you think Grampy knows what's going on?"

"Well, Abby, it is what they call a progressive disease and slowly the things people remember diminish. Yet sometimes they can surprise us with what they say. It is best if you try and remember that lovely man who took you on long walks by the river when you were younger and made you laugh."

Abby felt a strange sensation as her mum spoke; it was a mixture of a tremble and an aching running through her whole body. She couldn't say anything, so she just looked out of the window and tried to remember those walks her mum had mentioned. She could now see clearly one of those special walks where she was holding Grampy's hand; he had stopped and held his finger to his mouth and pointed to the path up ahead. She could remember being absolutely rooted to the spot as a straggly greyish brown animal as big as a dog moved across the path, it was sniffing and snuffling at the ground. It was soon followed by four smaller animals that were a lighter ginger-brown colour with thin black stripes running across their bodies. The animals crossed the path and soon disappeared into the bracken and woodland. She remembered clearly the thrill of seeing those creatures, and her grandfather saying they were wild boar. She hadn't thought about that moment for a long time; it was the only time she had ever seen these creatures. She now recalled her grandfather had told her all about them. Those words now echoed around her head.

"Wild boar live in woods and forests, and they are an ancestor of the pig. They once were extinct but for all sorts of reasons there are boar here in this forest; but you don't often see them. I often walk at night to try and see them."

As she looked out of the car window, watching the countryside flash past, she thought fondly of her grandfather and his love of wildlife.

"Mum, do you remember when I saw wild boar with Grampy?"

"Oh yes, I was so cross with him for taking you into the forest where wild boar roamed."

"He loves animals so I think he will like that home. It is just a pity that there isn't a pig there… because he does seem to have a thing about pigs, doesn't he?"

"Yes, he does, doesn't he? Not sure what started him off on that!"

Abby kept quiet now, but she reflected on those

special memories of her grandfather. She felt sad when she thought about how knowledgeable he had been about wildlife and how he was now. The idea that had been floating around in her head since the visit to the home now jumped out at her – almost hitting her between the eyes!

Grampy has this thing about pigs, so if that home had a pig, then maybe he would be able to settle down properly. I wonder if I can do something about that? Perhaps!

Abby used the journey to think about how she could get a pig to the nursing home and, of course, she had a particular pig in mind: old Herbert at Marie's farm! *I wonder how much a pig costs. Perhaps I could get enough money together to buy Herbert?*

When, after the interminable journey, they had unpacked, she quickly went round to see Marie at the farm.

*

Marie was pleased to see Abby.

"Marie, is Herbert still with you, and how are things on the farm now? When I spoke to you on the phone you said everything was going funny around the farm; is it OK now?"

"Well, the animals are certainly behaving differently. Dad is totally baffled by it all. Says he has never known anything like it in all his years. Yes, Herbert is still here. Dad hasn't had any time to do anything about Herbert yet since everything seemed to go haywire."

"How much would it cost to buy a pig like Herbert?"

"Why? Don't tell me you want to buy Herbert!"

Abby told Marie all about the care home and the animals.

"You see, Marie, that home would be perfect for Grampy; he has this thing about pigs and there is an empty sty there. I know pigs have a bit of a link with Gloucester in a funny sort of way."

She didn't mention that she thought Herbert had spoken to her – it wasn't the sort of thing you say to somebody: "Oh by the way your pig has been talking to me!"

Marie blurted out, "Well, not just because they're Gloucester Old Spot! You do know you get them all over the country not just Gloucester! It's just a well-known breed!"

"Yes, I know about them, but there is more to tell; while I was in Gloucester, I found out a story about a pig who sort of saved the city during the Civil War. The poor thing ended up dying but it managed to fool the King so that he didn't attack when he had the chance."

"Since when have you been so interested in history? I don't know anything about the Civil War stuff, but it seems to me that you are getting all soft and soppy about pigs! I will find out how much Dad thinks Herbert is worth. You know Dad can be funny about our animals; even though he is a farmer he gets very fond of them. Do you want to come and see old Herbert now?"

"Yes please – and Kenny of course."

They made their way down to where the stables and the sty were. Their way was blocked by a gaggle of geese who started hissing aggressively at them.

"I told you about the geese on the phone; this lot don't look that friendly. I'm just going back to get a pole so we can push them away without us getting hurt. I've had enough of being pecked at! You wait here, Abby."

Marie turned back to the house and jogged away.

Abby looked at the geese and was surprised to see them now turn away and waddle down to the pond. So Abby walked on to the stables by herself, keeping an eye on where the geese were, just in case. She smiled when she saw Kenny poking his head out of the stable; he neighed his greeting. She walked right up to the low sty wall and there was Herbert asleep lying on his side, his flanks rising and falling with his breathing.

She whispered, "Hello Herbert! It's me, Abby, you know, Marie's friend! The one you spoke to. I've just come back from Gloucester. Well, all sorts of strange things happened to me there. They all seem unbelievable and have confused me a bit, but I now know why you said Gloucester was a dangerous place for pigs. Although that was all a long, long time ago, of course; I am sure it is all OK now for pigs."

The pig hadn't moved at all and Abby felt silly talking to a sleeping pig. She looked round to check where Marie was. She could see her making her way back down, carrying a large pole. She turned back to Herbert.

"Look, I've got to be quick before Marie gets back. I don't want her to catch me talking to you. I've got a plan for you. I am going to try and raise money to buy you for a special home for people, and it has animals, and my grandad is going to go there. He loves pigs and he knows all about them – well he did once. It is near Gloucester, but I know you will be safe there. Well, it will be much safer than here!"

Abby noticed Herbert's ear lift up but there was no other movement. Marie had now arrived.

"What happened to the geese? Did I go all that way for nothing? I see you got here OK. You didn't get pecked then?"

"Well, almost as soon as you had gone back up, they turned round and waddled to the pond over there."

"That's typical! As I was coming back it looked like you were talking to Herbert. I'm always doing that to him and all the animals, especially Kenny."

For just a moment Abby hesitated; she thought for a moment that perhaps the animals talked to Marie as well. She wondered if she should say something, but luckily for her before she could open her mouth Marie carried on,

"Actually, even though I chat to them they are only really interested in what food I've got. I don't think it matters what I say to them! These geese are being really odd and aggressive these days. All the animals, as I said, have been strange and doing stuff you wouldn't expect over the last few days."

The pair of them now moved over to Kenny's stable. Kenny snorted at them.

"Charming!"

The pair of them stroked the horse's head.

"You are serious, aren't you, Abby, about Herbert and wanting to buy him?"

"Yes I am."

"Well, I'm fond of Herbert, he seems to have been around forever and I don't want him being turned into sausages!"

"Shush… don't say things like that here!"

Marie laughed.

Chapter 13

The Resistance (May 1944)

Holding the rifle was a young attractive woman; she was dressed in a green floral dress with a headscarf covering her dark hair. A terrified Tom raised his hands slowly and felt his legs wobble. She was studying him carefully, looking at his flying jacket and uniform. She spoke, "You are bloody lucky I didn't shoot you when I heard you creeping about. You bailed out last night?"

Tom was surprised to hear English with no accent at all and stared at her.

"Well?"

Tom hesitated; he knew he had to be careful and not give things away, and he just didn't know what to say.

"If you don't say anything, I will think you are some sort of spy, and your friends will be here in a minute. What's your name?"

"Sergeant Thomas Brown, RAF."

"You bailed out of that Lanc last night?"

"Sergeant Thomas Brown, RAF."

"So you are a bloody parrot, are you? Come on, you don't have to be a detective when you see a man in an RAF flying jacket with burn marks on it, looking like he has been dragged through a hedge backwards and also when a Lancaster crashed nearby, to work out you were part of the crew. Am I right, Thomas Brown?"

"Yes, and it's Tom."

"It is safer for all of us that you don't know my name."

"You're English?"

"Well, you could say I am bilingual, but I think my French might be wasted on you. It is best you don't know too much but you could be right."

"Patrick!"

Now a man emerged from the building. He was dressed in a labourer's jacket and had a navy-blue beret on his head. He was smiling broadly, and he was holding a pistol in his right hand.

"Bonjour, Monsieur."

"Hello… I mean bonjour, Patrick."

The woman spoke again. "We need to get you away from here, the place has been crawling with Krauts."

"Do you know if anyone else made it from the plane?"

"We know one was found by the Germans, but you're the first as far as I know who has been found by us. Now Patrick will take you to a safe place while we work out what to do with you. If you end up meeting a patrol Patrick might have to leave you to them; you should be all right in your uniform, but Patrick wouldn't be! Go!"

Patrick gestured for Tom to follow him and they moved back into the woods. After a stop-start journey they came to a farmyard. Tom was taken into the house where a woman was standing with a little girl. She smiled at him and gestured for him to sit at the table. Tom sat down and when bread, cheese and a mug of milk was put in front of him he wolfed the whole lot down.

"Thank you. I mean merci!"

Later he was taken to a small shed near the pigsty and given a blanket. Tom settled down and made himself comfortable. He stayed there for two days, keeping to his shed and coming out when summoned into the house, when it was dark, to have meals. They communicated through gestures and nods. Tom spent his hours in the shed using his knife to carve a small horse figure for the little girl. He was going to give it to her when he left.

One morning he was just settling down in his shed to carry on with his carving when he heard the unmistakable sound of a lorry approaching. It could only mean one thing – they had been betrayed! He had to get away. He moved to the door and ducked down, knowing he had to find a place to hide quickly. It was too late; the lorry was almost there. He couldn't risk running for it as he would be seen and he would be

a sitting duck. He jumped over the low wall into the pigsty. The large pig grunted but didn't move. He dived behind the pig and pulled some stinking straw over himself; he hoped it would be enough. He heard the lorry screech, there were bangs and the air was a hubbub of sound and menace. He heard a scream and more shouts. The little girl's crying was unbearable, but he knew if he showed himself it would be worse for the family. He heard the crack of another shot and more screams. His body was shaking but he stayed behind the sleeping pig, who hadn't reacted at all to his presence.

More shots rang out, and then came the deadly rat-a-tat of a machine gun. Bullets were being sprayed all over the farm. Tom squeezed down as much as he could behind the pig. The bullets were getting closer. He heard some thud into the roof of the sty. More screams. More bullets fizzed through the air. Tom was sweating; a gun started firing close to the sty. The pig grunted and wriggled. Bullets now crashed all around, splinters flew, and bullets now thudded into the pig's body; the pig shuddered and now stopped moving. Tom lay there; he heard some shouts and some banging and crashing from the lorry. He heard the lorry's engine revving its way up the hill from the farm. He still didn't move. Flies buzzed all around the pig's body. He was aware of something wet on his hand. He looked to see blood oozing from the pig onto his hand. It was all quiet apart from the buzzing flies. Tom eventually raised himself up. The pig was motionless, and Tom noticed it was riddled with bullet holes. He looked down at his hand; he was still holding the wooden horse he had been carving for the little girl. Tears streamed down his face. He bent down and touched the pig's head and, not sure why he did it, he said, "Thank you."

Chapter 14

Fate at the Fete?

When Abby got home, she checked the savings that she had at the Post Office. She had £262.50; she had been saving all her birthday money and Christmas money for something special. This was special! Marie had found out from her dad that Herbert might be worth about £425.

How am I going to raise that sort of money?

She searched around her room to see what things she might be able to sell. She couldn't really see anything that would raise much. She would have to talk to her mum and tell her about her plan.

Her mum listened carefully as Abby told her what she was planning to do (she didn't mention anything about her recent night-time adventures in Gloucester or the talking Herbert. Her mum would only think she was losing it).

"You are going to use all the money you have saved?"

Abby nodded.

Her mum smiled at her kindly.

"Well, that is a lovely thought, Abby, but I don't think the people who gave you the money thought you would use it to buy a pig. That money was meant for you, Abby."

Abby was annoyed with her mother.

"But that's what I want to do! It's my money – I can do what I want with it!"

As she stormed up towards her bedroom, she knocked over a stack of magazines. She slowly put them away, but she noticed something on the cover of one of them. It had cheerful pictures of knitted farm animals on it; there in the middle of the cover was a pink pig. Granny Sue had taught her to knit a couple of years ago and despite all the chaos when she had been in Gloucester, they had found some time to sit and knit together when Grampy had been sleeping. She quickly tidied up the mess but took the magazine into her room. She flicked to the pages about the knitted animals; she glanced over the knitting patterns.

"That's it! I could knit some of these and we could sell them to raise money to help send Herbert to Gloucester! I'm sure Granny will knit some animals as well and I might even get some friends to help."

It took a few phone calls to her friends and her granny; and a few visits to people who said they would donate wool. In no time at all she had a number of people knitting. She even persuaded her mum to knit as well, and quickly pigs, goats, geese and sheep were beginning to appear. Marie's dad even agreed to wait a bit longer before he sold Herbert, to give them time to raise the money.

One of her neighbours, Ruth Bayliss, who worked for the local radio station, was intrigued to see Abby and Marie knitting on a park bench.

"What are you doing?"

"We are knitting to send Herbert to Gloucester!"

Ruth listened to Abby, who told the story about her

grandfather and about the much-loved pig on Marie's farm; Abby even told Ruth the story that a pig had died saving Gloucester, thinking it might be a good story for the radio. Ruth agreed and was very keen for Abby to tell her story, so she quickly arranged everything. As she finished the broadcast, Abby told the radio listeners that the knitted animals would be a great present for young ones.

After the radio piece had been broadcast there were more offers of help and a place was given for them to have a table at the town fete to sell their knitted animals. Paolo, who was in Abby and Marie's class, said his dad, who ran an ice cream business, would give them some ice cream to sell; and lend them one of his special bikes that had a cool box on it. Surely now they could raise enough money for Herbert. Abby had also realised she would need some more money to hire someone to drive Herbert; this would mean a special trailer so Herbert could travel safely. She thought that might be expensive.

On the day of the fete Abby woke early and was both excited and nervous. The noise of rain rattling against her window made her look out. It was pouring in great torrents from leaden grey skies.

"Oh no!"

At breakfast her mum spoke gently to Abby.

"I'm sorry, love, I think they will have to call off the fete; this rain is torrential, and it doesn't look like stopping. Thunder and lightning are expected later, and they are worried the river might burst its banks in the town and cause some flooding."

"It can't be that bad, can it?"

"I think they have to think about safety for everybody. It is a pity because people have worked so hard getting everything ready."

"But they can't! I need to sell the animals! We need it for Herbert so he can go to the home for Grampy. He is supposed to be moving there next week, he needs a pig to look at! He will need it to help him settle in properly!"

Her eyes filled with tears.

"I'm sure Grampy will enjoy all the other animals there, he won't know there was going to be a pig there. You can still raise money to get Herbert there afterwards."

"It will be too late! Marie's dad will have to sell Herbert if we don't get the money for him. Marie's dad needs the sty for some piglets!"

"Well perhaps you can get another pig if Herbert has to be sold, maybe a couple of piglets even."

"Oh, Mum, it has to be Herbert. I promised!"

"I'm sure Marie's dad will understand."

Abby nearly said it wasn't Marie's dad she had promised but Herbert himself!

"No, it has to be Herbert! I told Granny Sue on the phone to tell Grampy all about Herbert!"

"Grampy won't know or remember, love; I think sometimes he doesn't even know us anymore."

The fete, of course, was called off; it had rained non-stop all day and only stopped later in the evening. The next morning Abby was sitting on the stairs looking at the great sack with all the animals they had knitted lying by the front door. Her mum had just gone to the shops.

What am I going to do now? I need to think of something.

She shut her eyes to think at the same moment the nearby church bell chimed ten o' clock.

Chapter 15

Relief!

Abby was surprised to hear lots of shouting and cheering.

She opened her eyes; she was no longer on her stairs at home but was sitting on a stone staircase! People all around her were dressed in those familiar old-fashioned clothes she had seen before and were moving quickly towards an even bigger crowd. She could hear the steady rhythm of beating drums getting gradually closer.

The grubby smiling face of John Ryan loomed up in front of her.

"You coming, Abigail?"

"Coming where?"

"You can be a silly oaf at times! To see Essex's army, of course! Come on, you can 'ear their drums. I want to see 'em march in."

He started to move with the crowd. Abby got up and followed John.

"John! Hang on! What happened to the King's army?"

"You are funny; I think your head needs sorting out! Remember they left a couple of days ago, when they knew Essex was almost 'ere. They couldn't cope with all that rain – it stopped them digging any tunnels and stuff. I reckon old Massey did a good job for us, even if he is a bit stuck up! 'E kept them on their toes!"

Abby knew all too well about the rain, but she didn't say anything because she didn't want to look even more stupid!

There were people milling around Eastgate as some soldiers were opening the great heavy wooden gates. The drums didn't let up and the noise reverberated all around.

Abby and John had squeezed to the front of the crowd and could see Colonel Massey wearing a black hat, striding forwards with two soldiers walking behind him. Cheers broke out on both sides of him. He was smiling and nodding appreciatively at the crowd. As he drew close to John and Abby he stopped and looked at them both.

"Well, John Ryan and Abigail Brown. Glad you haven't got yourselves in any more trouble. You see, Miss Brown, that pig you made all that fuss about has helped to save the city!"

Abby was about to open her mouth and speak up for the pig, but a shout rang out.

"Here they are!"

An important-looking soldier riding a large white horse was entering through the gate. He was dressed in a type of black tunic covered with a breastplate; he also wore a helmet and a sword dangled from his waist. He was followed by a squadron of cavalry. Each soldier was smartly dressed in a yellow coat that came down almost to the knees, a breastplate with a large brown belt fixed diagonally across the chest and a helmet with three bars at the front. They in turn were followed by ten drummers playing their constant rattling beat; behind them marched many soldiers, some carrying muskets and others great long pikes. The man on the horse now held his hand up. The drummers stopped and the army came to a halt. Colonel Massey left the children and walked up to the horse; he removed his hat and bowed to the man on the horse. Abby could hear everything that was being said.

"Welcome to Gloucester, my Lord Essex. I am Colonel Massey, and I have been in charge of the city forces. We are mighty pleased to see you."

"Colonel Massey, you and the city have done well to stand against the tyrant. Tell me what your situation is, and what news of the King's army?"

The Earl of Essex now dismounted and went over to shake Massey's hand.

"We are almost out of powder; we have only three barrels left and almost no food; the men are exhausted but have shown great valour. We think the King withdrew on news of your arrival. My scouts tell me he has moved off towards Painswick."

"Excellent news! Now, my men will need to be billeted and we need to make sure we arrange pickets just in case they come back and try and catch us unprepared."

Orders were given and the army gradually moved into the city, watched by the crowds. Massey and Essex had walked back to Massey's headquarters.

John tugged Abby's sleeve.

"Come on, we's can go outside properly now! No one is going to stop us now!"

Abby and John now moved to the open gate. It was the first time Abby had seen the area outside of the city in daylight and couldn't believe what she saw. Immediately outside of the gates and walls was a scene of complete devastation; the ground was black, burnt, from where houses had been set alight so the King's men would have no cover. In the distance they could see the remains of the King's camp, rubbish strewn everywhere. There were places where mud and soil were piled high, clearly where digging had taken place.

"That must be where they were digging a tunnel, but I heard it got flooded by all that rain!"

Abby suddenly gasped as she saw a body lying face down in water. She wanted to get away but how? She wished she was back home. She certainly wasn't keen to see any more horrors.

"I'm going to go back to see what's happening in the city."

"I ain't! I's going to see what I can find! There should be good stuff to pick up, before anyone else gets it!"

He reached down for a belt buckle and they both could see some things glinting up ahead of them. They were now aware that they weren't the only ones looking for anything that might be valuable. Three men, dressed in ragged clothing, were moving threateningly towards them. Abby could see they were armed with knives. She decided they wouldn't be that friendly and would take anything they had!

"Abigail, run! Grab what's on the ground!"

They rushed to where there were some glinting objects lying; they grabbed the objects on the run, and both started to hurtle back towards the city before the armed men knew what was happening. When they got back into the city there were soldiers milling around so they knew they were safe from the cutthroats outside. Their hearts were still thumping, and they were gasping for breath. John smiled.

"Those cutthroats were looking for things like this and they would just stick you to get anything valuable! What did you get?"

Abby held her hand open; she had grabbed a delicate gold ring off the ground.

"Good one, you can sell that! Look at what I've got!"

He opened his fist and showed her two silver coins.

"Half a crown and a tanner; that will get me some decent food and stuff now! Fancy it just lying there waiting for us! I'm rich now, ain't I?"

With that John dashed off to find something to spend his coins on. Abby started to walk towards the cathedral, holding her ring. Her legs ached with her efforts and she looked for somewhere to rest. She was by an old house that had been damaged by cannon fire, and she sat down on the rubble of one of the walls. She looked carefully at the ring she had picked up. It was delicate and had a red jewel in the centre. She wondered how it had ended up lying in the mud.

Perhaps they were in such a rush and somebody just dropped it? I wonder if they have missed it. If I was at home, I would have given it in to the police or something. What should I do with it? It isn't mine!

She was uncomfortable with this booty. She could see soldiers moving around near Massey's headquarters and she saw Massey standing surveying the damage to the houses nearby. Without really thinking she moved towards him and nobody stopped her.

"Colonel Massey!"

He turned and looked at her.

"Miss Brown, we meet again. I hope you are not going to admonish me again about that blessed pig?"

"No, sir. Well, just now we were outside the walls near the King's camp. And I found something. I'm not sure what to do with it."

"You and the King's camp again! Perhaps you really are a spy, after all?"

She could tell by his tone that he wasn't serious.

"Well, what did you find?"

She held out her palm with the ring on it. Massey took it, studied it, and looked thoughtfully at Abby.

"Well, it is the sort of ring that a gentleman would wear. Why are you asking me about it?"

"Well, it isn't mine, so I didn't know what to do with it. Who should I give it to?"

Massey threw his head back and roared with laughter.

"You are a strange one and yet an honest one. Look, war is a terrible thing and in war things are lost and found. You have found this, Miss Brown; and as far as I can see it is yours, unless you are thinking of following the King and asking everyone in his army if it is their ring? It would take a long time and they might think you were a spy once again, just like I did!"

Abby turned the ring over in her hand and looked up at Colonel Massey.

"Just doesn't feel right."

"Miss Brown, your honesty is admirable. You now have the ring. I think you should use it for something that matters or give it as a gift. There may well be a time in the future when that ring might come in useful."

Colonel Massey turned and walked back to his headquarters, leaving Abby; she went back to her perch on the rubble, not sure what to do next.

The bells behind her started to chime the hour. She thought she knew what would happen next so she shut her eyes. Nothing happened; she was still sitting on the rubble, holding the ring in her palm and she felt panic rising up through her body.

What happens if I'm stuck here unable to get back to my time?

She stood up, clenching the ring in her hand, and looked around. Colonel Massey had disappeared, soldiers were milling around and there was no sign of John Ryan. What should she do, how was she going to get back to her time? She now noticed an old man sitting on another bit of debris. He wore a dirty grey smock and had a battered old hat perched at an angle on his head; he was staring straight ahead. Abby was worried that something was wrong because he was so still; for a moment she worried if he was even breathing.

"Excuse me, are you all right?"

The old man turned and looked blankly at Abby.

"No, I's not… got nothing left, has I? All gone, ain't it? None left now! My poor lovelies!"

"What's gone?"

"My poor lovelies! Watched them be born and grow I have!"

She thought this man wasn't quite there. She smiled at him.

"What are your lovelies? I don't understand."

"My pigs, all gone, no more."

The penny now dropped with Abby.

"You're a pig farmer?"

"None left at all, last one they took the other night, said they wanted to borrow it, but it died, and they never brought it back. I was going see that Massey fellow about it. Ain't right! Don't know what I'm going to do now."

"I saw them with your pig, they squeezed it to death to fool the King. I told them to stop!"

"Finished I is, finished! I's been doing pigs all my life. Only know about pigs do I, nothing else. That's it! Gone!"

A tear ran down his stubbly chin. Abby felt for the old man, she wanted to help him. Her hand was hurting, the ring had pressed deep into the palm of her hand. The ring! It was no good to her, was it? Massey had told her it was valuable, but she didn't want it, because it didn't feel right.

"Here, have this; I found it outside the walls."

She pushed the ring into the old man's hand. He looked at her quizzically.

"For me? Why?"

"A man's ring is no good for me. Use it to buy another pig!"

The old man examined the ring, turning it over and over. He smiled at her, showing his teeth with several gaps in.

"Thank you kindly, my dear, I's will get me more than one pig. I should think it will get a few!"

Just at that minute Abby felt dizzy. Now she knew what was coming; she smiled with relief and shut her eyes.

Chapter 16

Can Pigs Really Fly?

The phone ringing made her open her eyes. She was still sitting on the stairs.

"Hello?"

"Hello, Abby, it's me, Granny Sue; is your mum there?"

Abby remembered her mum had gone down to the shop.

"I've got a date for your grandpa; it is next Saturday. How did the fete go – did you get enough money selling the knitted toys?"

"No, it rained so much the fete was cancelled. I am thinking of holding a tabletop sale outside the house, but it won't be as good as the fete with all those people that would have been around."

"Oh dear. I was hoping you might have got the pig sorted for when your grandad goes to the home.

He keeps talking about pigs all the time, it seems to be morning, noon and night!"

Abby winced when she heard this. So she blurted out without thinking, "Don't worry Granny, we will get Herbert there somehow."

There was a pause at the other end before her Granny spoke again.

"Abby, actually I have something here that might help. Grampy always said it was for you. You see he has two really old coins here that he and his friend, who had one of those metal detector thingies, found. Grampy thinks they must have come from the Siege of Gloucester because they have Charles the First's head on them. I know that he wanted you to have them."

Abby gasped with surprise, "What?"

"Yes, he had two special coins that he thought must have come from the time of the siege. I think they found them somewhere near the Priory before those new houses were built."

"Are you sure Grampy would want them to go? What type of coins are they?"

"Well, you won't know these coins because they are old money, what we used when I was a girl. One is half a crown and the other is a sixpence we used to call—"

"A tanner!"

"Yes, that's right. How do you know that?"

Abby smiled as she answered, "Oh, we did something about old money at school."

"Well, I think if we sell them you should get a couple of hundred pounds. That would really help get Herbert here, I should think."

"That's great, Granny, but are you sure?"

"Well, I don't think Grampy would mind. He hasn't looked at them for ages; all he seems to be interested in is blessed pigs!"

When Abby had said goodbye on the phone, she just sat there thinking about all that had happened. *This is all getting silly, it can't be, surely? Maybe we can do it after all*.

Her mum arrived home and Abby told her about the phone call.

"I will just phone her back. She will be getting worried about Dad; it is such a big step for her."

Abby spent the time whilst her mum was on the phone working out if she had enough money. Her mum was upset when she finally said goodbye on the phone and Abby threw her arms around her. The doorbell rang. Her mum wiped her tears away.

"I wonder who that can be?"

She went and opened the door. Standing in front

of her was a man dressed in green overalls, a flat cap perched on his head (it was slightly crooked) and he was wearing wellies. A large red tractor was parked out on the road outside.

"You be Abby's mum?"

Abby's mum wondered for a moment if something was wrong.

"Well, I be Marie's father from up at the farm."

"Oh yes, they are good friends."

Abby had come to the door and smiled. "Hello, Mr Preece!"

"Hello there, well I've come about old Herbert!"

"Oh, Mr Preece, I am still trying to get the money together. I might need a few more days."

"I does not want your money."

Abby began to panic.

"Please just a couple more—"

"I doesn't want your money; you can have him."

"Pardon?"

"You can have him. Marie tells me your grandfather likes pigs?"

"Yes, he does."

Abby's mother now spoke. "Mr Preece, do I understand this right, you are giving us Herbert?"

"Yes."

"Err, err, thank you, that is very generous."

Abby now asked, "We will try and sort out coming to get him – but why aren't you going to sell him?"

Mr Preece paused and looked uncomfortable.

"Well, it's a long story and you mustn't laugh. You see when Marie told me about your grandfather in Gloucester it got me thinking. See, I'm fond of old Herbert, shouldn't be daft like that or soft, what with me being a farmer. It reminded me of an old family story that my grandfather used to tell me when I was a boy."

Abby's mum interjected, "Would you like to come in and have a cup of tea?"

"No thanks, I'm a bit messy…"

He pointed to his mud-splattered wellies.

"As I was saying, my grandfather was a farmer. All my family have been farmers since forever and he said that our forebears lived in Gloucester before we moved east to here. Seems funny now, our family seemed to have been in these parts here forever! Well, so the story goes, my ancestor was a pig farmer in Gloucester when the country was at war with itself."

"The Civil War?"

"Aye, and he was down on his luck; all his pigs were gone. So the story goes, his last one was squeezed to death by the soldiers to fool the King and save the city.

And it worked; but it was his last pig and he had not a penny to his name!"

Abby was incredulous as Mr Preece was telling his story.

"Anyway, he had nothing left after the siege but then someone just gave him a ring which they'd found; it was supposed to be valuable. Anyhow with it he was able to buy himself a whole lot of pigs when the war was finally over. The family never looked back after that. So I figures I should give something in a good cause myself, especially as I heard it was Gloucester – though I've never been there! And I figures it might help with the stuff going on at the farm at the moment."

Abby felt a shiver and the hairs on the back of her neck stood on end.

Her mum spoke, "That is a lovely story and as I said, very generous, isn't it, Abby?"

Abby's mouth was wide open, and her mother had to nudge her.

"Isn't it, Abby, it is very generous!"

"Er erm… yes, thank you, yes… that is amazing! Thanks."

"Well, there you are and don't you worry about how to move Herbert. I will do it if you give me the address."

"Thank you!"

*

It was all sorted; Mr Preece did take Herbert to the home, where they were delighted to see him. Abby decided with her mum and friends that she would still sell the knitted animals and that the money raised would go to the Alzheimer's Society.

The day before her grandfather was due to go to the home, they set off to Gloucester to support Granny Sue. Abby was reassured when she saw the great tower of the cathedral standing out above the other buildings as they approached the city. She thought to herself, as her mum drove towards her grandparents' house, *I've seen that from many different angles and different times recently, but it still is the same cathedral! I think!*

Chapter 17

Home

The following morning everyone was anxious about how it would all go. Abby's grandfather was wandering around the garden and didn't want to go and get in the car. Granny Sue and her mum were both upset and were struggling to cajole him from the garden. Abby went up to him; she saw he was holding a small carved wooden horse.

"You've got a horse, Grampy. Where did that come from?"

Granny Sue spoke through her tears.

"It was his father's; he made it in the war and George always kept it safe in his old tobacco tin. It was like his treasure. Funny, he went to get it this morning of all mornings. Hasn't touched it for ages."

Abby smiled.

"So it *is* precious then! A special one! Grampy, look what I've got for you, this is a special one too!"

She showed him one of the knitted pigs that she had brought especially for him.

He took it in his hand and his whole face creased in a smile.

"Piggy!"

"Yes, it is. Grampy, shall we go see a pig now?"

He pushed the horse into Abby's hand, and she took it.

"Yours now!"

With her other hand she took his free hand and led him from the garden through the house to the car. When they got to the home everyone was kind and welcoming. Abby had insisted that his special coins (the half crown and the sixpence) were displayed in a lovely case that went into his room. Her grandfather wasn't interested in the room at all but kept asking, "Piggy, Piggy?"

"Of course, Grampy. Come on, let's go and see Herbert the pig."

They held hands and walked to where all the farm animals were kept at the end of the garden. Her mum and Granny followed behind. Chickens were clucking and a donkey stood patiently in a fenced paddock looking straight ahead. But they were only interested in going to the sty.

They could see the great heavy pinkish body with the distinctive black spots lying on its side, sleeping. When they approached, Herbert opened his eyes and Grampy smiled.

"Piggy, piggy!"

"Yes, it is! His name is Herbert. He is a Gloucester Old Spot; he had to be, didn't he? You can come here and see him whenever you are in the garden."

Abby looked over at Herbert and whispered, "You're safe now. You won't believe what has happened to me recently and the journey I've been on to get you here!"

Herbert looked at her blankly and Abby swore he gave her a wink; she wasn't sure, but nothing would surprise her anymore!

Her grandfather looked around and spoke.

"Elephant, where is it?"

Abby laughed.

"If you think I'm getting you an elephant…"

She thought, *Well, that might be a different sort of adventure but where on earth would you put it?*

Postscript

I first came across the legend of the 'Gloucester Pig' in Merlin Price's book *Folktales and Legends of Gloucestershire*. You can also find references to a pig saving the city all over the internet. There is no clue to what type of pig it was, so of course I decided that the pig had to be Gloucester Old Spot – it couldn't be anything else, could it? In my research the lines between the Civil War forces were often porous so I thought John and Abby's foray could have happened. The King's forces besieging Gloucester were hampered both by bad weather (their tunnel to mine the city walls did get flooded) and Colonel Massey's many sorties. Charles was reluctant to attack.

The Humpty Dumpty nursery rhyme has been associated with the siege; this is because the big siege gun that was brought in from the Netherlands did explode on its first shot from near Llanthony Secunda Priory, about half a mile from the city centre. The nursery rhyme is also associated with Colchester; but despite these claims the reality is that the origin of the rhyme is unknown.

The strand of the story from the Second World War with the Lancaster flying over occupied Europe just before D-Day is possible because there were many raids in and around D-Day. Many Lancasters were lost and sadly when a plane was hit many were unable to bail out. The command 'Abracadabra' in the story came from one account I read. It gave some clarity for the whole crew; when they heard the word 'Abracadabra' they knew it was the bail out code. The shooting around the farm idea came from reading about the terrible fate of the villagers of Oradour-sur-Glane in 1944.

Finally, Alzheimer's is a disease we are all aware of and many of us have experienced friends and family who are dealing with it or have dealt with it. I didn't want to make light of it when the grandfather keeps talking about piggies, etc. However, I was profoundly moved on one of my storytelling visits to a dementia unit. As I was telling my stories I could see two members of my audience holding mini toy farm animals, another was holding a doll and one had a small racing car. Who knows one might have been holding a carved wooden horse!

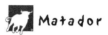